## "I've Applie~~d~~

Isabel announced.

Craig's mouth dropped open. "Oh, Isabel, I think that's great."

"You do?"

"You'll make a wonderful mother for her."

"Tell that to the state," she said glumly.

"Is there a problem?"

"Yes, a big one. There's another couple that's been on the list for a baby girl for a long time."

"But they wouldn't take Sandy away from you, would they?"

Isabel hesitated. "They might. You see, they have something important that I'm lacking."

"What's that?"

When she answered, her words were barely audible. "A father."

Dear Reader,

This month we're filled with fabulous heroes, delightful babies, tie-in stories and a touch of the magical!

The MAN OF THE MONTH, *Mr. Easy*, is from one of your favorites, Cait London, who once again spins a love story in her own special way.

Next, we have *babies*. First, in *The Perfect Father*, another installment in the FROM HERE TO MATERNITY series by Elizabeth Bevarly, and next in Karen Leabo's wonderful *Beach Baby*.

For those of you who have been looking for the next episode of Suzanne Simms's HAZARDS, INC. series, look no more! It's here with *The Maddening Model*.

Peggy Moreland brings us a hero with a mysterious past—and a heroine with a scandalous ancestress—in *Miss Lizzy's Legacy*. And don't miss the very special *Errant Angel* by award-winning author Justine Davis.

This month—as with every month—if you want it special, sexy and superb, you'll find it…in Silhouette Desire.

Happy reading!

Lucia Macro
Senior Editor

Please address questions and book requests to:
Silhouette Reader Service
U.S.: 3010 Walden Ave., P.O. Box 1325, Buffalo, NY 14269
Canadian: P.O. Box 609, Fort Erie, Ont. L2A 5X3

# KAREN
# LEABO
## BEACH BABY

SILHOUETTE *Desire*®
Published by Silhouette Books
America's Publisher of Contemporary Romance

SILHOUETTE BOOKS

ISBN 0-373-05922-1

BEACH BABY

Copyright © 1995 by Karen Leabo

This edition published by arrangement with Harlequin Enterprises B.V.

® and TM are trademarks of Harlequin Enterprises B.V., used under
license. Trademarks indicated with ® are registered in the United States
Patent and Trademark Office, the Canadian Trade Marks Office and in
other countries.

Printed in U.S.A.

**Books by Karen Leabo**

## *KAREN LEABO*

credits her fourth-grade teacher with initially sparking her interest in creative writing. She was determined at an early age to have her work published. When she was in the eighth grade, she wrote a children's book and convinced her school yearbook publisher to put it in print.

Karen was born and raised in Dallas. She has worked as a magazine art director, a free-lance writer and a textbook editor, but now she keeps herself busy writing full-time about romance.

# One

Isabel turned on the nursery lamp, picked up the squalling infant and cuddled it. "Don't cry, little man. Aunty Isabel is here," she cooed as she gently rocked the tiny bundle. His crying only increased in volume as his face turned to crimson. Sometimes she felt so helpless because she couldn't give him what he wanted.

A shadow moved through the doorway. "Isabel." The single word was filled with censure.

"He was crying," Isabel said defensively, clutching the baby more tightly.

"I heard him. I'm here." Isabel's younger sister, Angie, held out her arms. "Give him to me."

Isabel felt an insane urge to flee with the child. Twenty-year-old Angie hadn't even wanted him, not at first. Isabel hesitated a fraction of a second before handing the baby to his mother.

Soon Angie was settled in a rocking chair, the baby suckling greedily at her swollen breast. "*I'm* his mother, not you," she said softly. "I'm grateful for all the help you've given me. I don't know where I'd be if you hadn't let me live here and work for you. But it's time for you to back off. How can I learn anything about being a mother if you're always rushing in to take care of Corey before I can get there? It's a good thing I'm the one producing milk, or I'd never get to hold him."

Isabel bit her lower lip. Angie was right. Throughout her little sister's pregnancy, and especially after she'd brought Corey home from the hospital, Isabel had taken charge. She had forced Angie to eat balanced meals and get her rest, made sure she got to her doctor's appointments and had paid for everything. She had bought a crib and clothes and diapers for the baby and had decorated the nursery—all the while feeling sick with envy.

The thing she wanted most in life was to raise a child. But at age thirty she still had no babies of her own. She'd simply never met the man she wanted to marry, and she refused to bring a life into the world without a loving father. It was hard to accept that Angie, who until two weeks ago didn't have a maternal bone in her young body, was happily settling into motherhood.

"I'm sorry, sis," Isabel whispered, her throat clogged with tears. "I thought I was helping."

Angie softened. "You are. All I'm asking for is a chance to try being Corey's mom. I may not do everything right—"

"You're doing great, kiddo." Isabel lightly touched the peach fuzz on Corey's bald head. "I'm really going to miss you two."

"We're only moving a couple of blocks away. And guess who my favorite baby-sitter will be?"

"I think Mom and I will have to arm wrestle for the privilege." Isabel managed a smile. Angie was trying to make amends for her earlier sharp words, but there was nothing to forgive as far as Isabel was concerned. She'd deserved worse for being such an interfering aunt.

As Angie returned her attention to her nursing son, Isabel slipped out, closing the nursery door quietly behind her.

She would never be able to sleep, she decided. It was after five, anyway. She might as well get dressed and start out early for her morning run.

She climbed into a pair of old sweats and pulled her thick, dark brown hair into a crooked ponytail. The sun wasn't up yet. Who would see her?

She tiptoed down the creaky, front staircase of the Victorian "painted lady," which housed her business in addition to being her home. The many rooms in the huge old house were perfect for showcasing her interior-design skills to potential clients.

At the bottom of the stairs she gave the intricately carved newel a pat. She had put so much love into this house. Not one detail had been overlooked. It was as beautiful, warm and comfortable as a home could be. Now all it lacked was the ring of a child's laughter.

Corey's presence had given Isabel a tantalizing taste of motherhood. But he and his mother were moving out tomorrow. Chafing at her big sister's interference, Angie had impulsively put a deposit down on a ramshackle apartment she could barely afford. But Angie, as always, went her own way. She would manage somehow.

After putting on a pot of coffee, Isabel set out for the Galveston Island beach five blocks away. The morning was nippy, although the start of spring was officially only days away. She tucked her hands under the hem of her sweatshirt until her brisk walking warmed her up. When she hit the sand she began to run, slowly at first, gradually stretching her muscles. She concentrated on her breathing. In—out—in—out. The tension caused by her encounter with Angie began to seep away.

Isabel's pleasantly drifting thoughts were suddenly interrupted by a foreign noise. She slowed and cocked her head, straining to listen above the gentle roar of waves. It had sounded like a baby.

There! She heard it again. What would a baby be doing on a dark beach?

"Iz, you're losing it," she muttered with a shake of her head as she resumed running. She had babies on the brain! From the moment of Corey's arrival, she had tuned into the noises he made. The slightest gurgle could wake her from a sound sleep.

This noise was probably a cat, she concluded.

When she heard it again, she slid to a stop. That was no cat. She followed the sound of the pitiful wailing. When she found the source, a rush of conflicting emotions rose in her throat until she could hardly breathe. There, lying on an old newspaper, was a newborn infant, barely hours old.

Isabel's first instinct was to snatch up the baby and hold its chilled body in her trembling arms. She did just that as rage and compassion warred inside her. "Who would *do* this?" she cried aloud. To discard a helpless human life as if it were yesterday's garbage was the most heinous crime she could envision.

For several seconds she stood paralyzed by the fury she felt toward the baby's mother. But finally sanity reasserted itself. She had to get this tiny scrap of humanity to a hospital, and fast. No telling how long she had lain there, naked, exposed to the cool night wind and dampness, hungry and possibly injured.

She tucked the baby securely under her sweatshirt, where she could be warmed by Isabel's body heat. Then she ran for a nearby stairway that ascended from the beach to Seawall Boulevard.

At this hour, the street was deserted with the exception of one set of headlights coming her way. Since this might be her fastest route to medical care, she stood in the middle of the street, holding the baby with one hand and waving frantically at the approaching car with the other.

Craig Jaeger's mind was on the meeting scheduled for later that morning. He was so intent on mentally reviewing his presentation that he didn't see the wraith-like figure, dressed all in black, that jumped out in front of him until it was almost too late.

He jammed on the brakes, and still he would have hit her if she hadn't skittered out of the way.

Belatedly he honked the horn. "Lady, are you out of your mind?" he called out the open window of his BMW. "I could have killed you."

She wasted no time arguing and, instead, jerked the passenger door open and jumped inside. "Please, I need help." Her voice was clear, her words calm, but her brown eyes were wide with fright. She bent slightly at the waist as she clutched at her stomach. "You have to take me to a hospital. I have a newborn baby here."

The shock of her words was like a splash of ice water in Craig's face. He put the car in gear and hit the gas. "My God, you just gave birth and you're running around in the street?"

"It's not *my* baby. Do you know where the St. Augustus Hospital is?" she demanded.

"Yes. Whose baby is it?"

"I don't know. I found her," she snapped.

"You're kidding."

"Would I make up something like that? I found her on the beach! Can't you drive this thing any faster?"

He was already exceeding the speed limit by a good fifteen miles per hour. To appease the mystery woman beside him, he made it twenty. She was positively vibrating with fury, but he recognized that at least the anger wasn't directed at him.

He chanced a look at her when he stopped for a light. She was striking, with her thick, dark brown hair pulling loose from a ponytail to frame her oval face. Her olive skin glowed from her recent exertions, her eyes were huge and ringed with long, dark lashes. Her lips were full and naturally pouty. She had an impudent little ski-slope of a nose that appeared strangely at odds with the sexy sophistication suggested by the rest of her face.

"The light's green!" she cried suddenly. "Go!"

Craig floored it. The woman might look like a sultry angel, but she had a voice that would put an army drill sergeant to shame.

The baby under her shirt made a fretful noise. She answered by cooing as she rocked it.

"Do you think the baby's okay?" he asked.

She turned to look at him, perhaps surprised by his show of concern. Until now he'd been too shocked to exhibit any. "I don't know," she said earnestly. "She's plenty big for a newborn, and she was crying, so I guess her lungs work."

"She's quiet now. I think she likes your voice." So did Craig. The tones were soft and musical—when she wasn't screaming at him. "You've had practice at this, I guess."

She looked down before answering. "I haven't found too many babies on the beach before. But my four-week-old nephew is living with me."

"So you're, what, like a nanny or something?"

"I was more like a mom until my sister got the hang of things." With her next words, the hard edge returned to her voice. "She doesn't have a husband. The slime disappeared the moment he found out Angie was pregnant." She paused, shaking her head. "I don't understand. I just don't get how anyone could—" Her intense gaze was suddenly focused on him. "Would you? Could you abandon your own child?"

He guessed that to answer *yes* would invite all sorts of mayhem. Fortunately he didn't have to. "No," he said in all honesty. This woman had no idea how sincerely he meant it. He'd seen firsthand what abandonment could do to a young psyche. Not that he or his younger brother had been left on a beach, but there were all kinds of ways to discard children.

The woman peeked under the sweatshirt to check on the foundling. A streetlight illuminated the baby's pink head covered with a light dusting of black hair. Craig also saw a strip of the woman's midriff.

"What's your name?" he asked, undeniably intrigued.

She surprised him by flashing a heart-melting smile. "Isabel. And since I've undoubtedly ruined your morning, you'll probably want to forget it as quickly as possible.''

"You didn't help my morning any," he admitted. "But I could hardly refuse to take a sick kid to the hospital." He didn't like disappointing the investors who'd hired him to build their luxury condominium complex, and he shuddered to think what his father would have to say. Sinclair Jaeger was just waiting for his son to falter.

"You'll be rid of us soon," Isabel said coolly. "The emergency room entrance is just past the next light."

"Yes, I see it."

"I do appreciate your help, no matter how grudging," she said. "I'm sorry I yelled at you... I told you my name, but I forgot to ask yours."

"Craig. Craig Jaeger."

Her brows drew together for a moment, and then her eyes lit up with recognition. "Ah, the architect. You're building the Blue Waters condos."

"That's right." He was surprised she'd heard of him. His name wasn't exactly a household word in Galveston.

"I'm in the design business," she explained.

Craig would have asked her more about her work, but there was no time. The hospital emergency entrance loomed before them. He pulled up in front of the double-glass doors, turned off the ignition and opened his door.

"You don't have to come with me," she said as she quickly slid out of the passenger seat.

The hell he didn't. He would never make it to the airport in time for his flight, anyway. He'd been running late before the wraith had waylaid him. Now that he'd become involved in this adventure, he felt a weird compulsion to see it through.

Isabel was surprised, but not displeased, that her reluctant knight wasn't ready to ride into the sunrise. In fact, she was extremely glad to have him there when he pushed his way into the ER and took charge. His commanding presence alone was enough to make people take notice, especially when he was wearing a no-nonsense power suit. But when he spoke in a quiet but authoritative voice, every nurse and doctor within a hundred yards strained to listen.

"We have a newborn baby here, found abandoned on the beach," he said to the triage nurse. "The child needs immediate attention."

"Yes, sir." The nurse issued a few terse orders of her own. Almost instantaneously an Isolette appeared.

Isabel pulled up her sweatshirt to reveal the infant that had been nestled so securely against her skin. The baby whimpered in protest, squeezing her eyes closed as if trying to shut out the cruel outside world.

The nurse gasped when she saw the condition of the child, as did Isabel. Under the bright hospital lights, it became apparent that she had never even been bathed after the birth.

"Merciful heavens," the nurse said under her breath.

Craig Jaeger uttered a slightly less pristine sentiment as he reached out and touched the infant's tiny hand. The simple gesture was filled with compassion. At that moment his eyes locked with Isabel's, and something passed between them, something every bit as strong and real as a blast of hot air from a furnace.

Isabel was so shaken, the nurse had to practically pry the baby out of her arms. She felt a stirring of separation anxiety. She had held the child in her arms for perhaps ten minutes, no more, but that was long enough. A bond had formed.

For a crazy moment, Isabel wondered if she was destined to spend her whole life handing babies over to other people. She chanced another look at Craig, but he seemed to be deliberately avoiding her gaze.

Pulling herself together, Isabel asked the nurse, "Is Dr. Keen working this morning?"

"Yes, he is," the nurse replied as she settled the baby into the Isolette. "You know Dr. Keen?"

"He's my nephew's pediatrician. Can you call him?"

"He's already been notified." With that, the nurse whisked the baby away, leaving Isabel feeling suddenly purposeless.

When she again looked at Craig, who was consulting his Rolex, she was able to pay more attention. He was tall and broad-shouldered, and his well-muscled body looked oddly out of place in that civilized suit and tie. His face, too, bore a ruggedness that suggested time spent in the great outdoors. He made her think of untamed wilderness, jungles and steep cliffs and tidal waves. And that hair, black as sin, was even darker than her own. She wondered if he had Hispanic roots, as she did.

When he looked up, their gazes locked again, and for one heart-stopping moment she thought he could read her thoughts, feel the emptiness she felt at having her found baby so suddenly jerked from her arms—and the pang of awareness, totally inappropriate, that she felt for him. But then the moment passed. His eyes were a steady slate blue.

"I think the admitting nurse wants to talk to us," he said, glancing over Isabel's shoulder.

Isabel turned to see the white-uniformed woman behind the admitting desk waving toward them. "We need to fill out papers."

Ah, of course. Red tape. Hospitals were full of it. "I can take care of it," she said to Craig. "If you need to go..."

He merely pursed his lips into a determined line and led the way to the desk, easing himself gracefully into one of the two plastic chairs. Isabel sank into the other one, not quite sure what to make of him.

"Could I have your name, please?" the grim-faced nurse began.

Before Isabel could even take a breath to answer, the man beside her replied, "Craig Jaeger. I'd like to take care of the hospital bill."

"Wait a minute!" she objected. "You don't have to do that. I can handle it."

"Hold it, hold it," the nurse interrupted. "An abandoned baby is a temporary ward of the state. Neither one of you has to pay for her medical treatment. I just need a name for the records."

"I'd still like to be responsible for the bill," Craig insisted. "Whatever she needs...I'll pay for it."

Isabel suspected the nurse hadn't often encountered such magnanimity. She wore a surprised look on her face as she took down the information Craig gave her.

"I'd like to help," Isabel said, feeling left out.

But Craig shook his head. "If I can't handle it, I'll let you know."

She got the impression that he would have no problem handling the bills. He carried that self-assuredness common to many of her wealthy clients.

"Now, then," the nurse said when she'd gotten all the financial information, "the patient's name. We'll just have to call her Jane Doe until we find out—"

"Sandy," Craig interrupted.

The nurse looked at him over the top of her reading glasses. Isabel, too, stared at him.

"It seems appropriate, since you found her in the sand," he said. "And anyway, my guess is she never had a name. Whoever abandoned her didn't think of her as human. They wouldn't have bothered to name her."

Isabel was frankly amazed that this man, who looked so harsh and uncompromising, would understand something so subtle as the humanizing act of awarding a name. Her curiosity about him grew.

The nurse looked to Isabel for a confirming nod, then grinned mischievously. So she did have a sense of humor. "Sandy it is," she said as she printed down the information.

When all forms were filled out in triplicate, Isabel thought she was done with all the questions. But as she stood up, she saw a uniformed officer from the Galveston police entering the ER.

"Are you the one who found the baby?" he asked.

She nodded.

Surprisingly, Craig still didn't take his leave, although he checked his watch on a regular basis. He remained by her side as the officer took them into the waiting room to ask questions.

"Now, exactly where on the beach did you find the infant?" the officer asked.

Isabel was at a loss. "It was somewhere between Eighteenth Street and the Hilton, but that's about two miles."

"You were right in front of the Texaco station when you flagged me down," Craig added.

"That's right, I remember now. The baby was lying near the seawall, just a few feet from that staircase across from the Texaco station."

The officer scribbled in his notebook.

"It was about ten minutes after six," Craig added. "I know, because I was running late." He flipped back his cuff and consulted his watch again. An irritated expression crossed his face.

"You don't have to stay," she said.

"I'll stay," he said grimly. "I just need to make a phone call." He appeared none-too-anxious to make that call. In fact, he stuck with her until the officer had finished his questions, only rising to find the phone when there was nothing left to be discussed.

She watched him walk away, thinking what a strange character he was. On one hand he was all stern and businesslike. Yet his compassion toward the abandoned baby was unmistakable. He didn't want to admit to any softness, but why would he stick around unless it was to make sure Sandy was doing all right?

"What will happen to her now?" Isabel asked the officer.

"We'll investigate as best we can," he replied. "Maybe someone at the gas station saw something. And I'm sure the paper and TV station will publicize the story, so that hopefully someone will come forward. Meanwhile, as soon as the baby is released from the hospital, social services will place her in foster care."

"But the parents..." Isabel persisted. "They won't get her back, will they?"

"Not likely," the officer said as he walked away, his voice reflecting the same disgust Isabel felt.

Craig hadn't returned by the time Dr. Keen made an appearance. Jonathan Keen was pushing retirement age, but he still put in his hours at the hospital. He had taken care of Isabel and all her younger siblings when they were children, and now he was working on a second generation of DeLeons. He was also a dear family friend.

"Oh, Dr. Keen," she said in a breathless rush, jumping out of her seat when she spotted him, with his familiar shock of white hair, at the waiting room door. "I'm so glad you were here. How's she doing?"

His smile was reassuring. "So, *you're* responsible for bringing her in. I might have known. She appears to be just fine—eight pounds, eight ounces of sugar and spice. My examination didn't reveal any abnormalities. Her lungs are clear and her reflexes are good."

Isabel was unutterably relieved. "Do you think she's Hispanic?" she asked. "I told the police officer as much."

Dr. Keen nodded. "Judging from her coloring, that would be my best guess."

Isabel worried her lower lip with her front teeth. "What if no one wants to adopt her?"

Dr. Keen patted her shoulder. "Don't worry, Isabel. A cute little mite like her, she won't lack for love. And speaking of cute little mites, how's Corey doing?"

She smiled warmly at the thought of her nephew, who had come into the world so loved, unlike Sandy. "He's fine. Angie's doing better, too. In fact, she told me this morning to butt out, that she was perfectly capable of taking care of her own son."

"That's quite a change of attitude."

Isabel huffed. "No kidding. When the nurse first put Corey in her arms, she looked at him like he was a space alien. Now she's positively doting."

"Does that bother you?"

"Frankly, yeah," Isabel admitted. "I'm jealous as hell."

"You, too, could be an unwed mother," he reminded her with a chuckle.

She shook her head. "That's not the way I want to do it. Say, Dr. Keen, do you think social services would let me foster this baby until she's adopted?"

He frowned and stroked his chin thoughtfully. "You've been a foster-mother before, right?"

"Yes..." After her one and only experience with a foster child, she had taken herself off the list. It had nearly torn her up when the court had returned the eight-year-old boy to his alcoholic mother, even if the mother had undergone treatment and taken a parenting class.

"Good foster homes are always in short supply," Dr. Keen said. "But you know how social services is. You have to go through channels and all that."

She sighed. "It's probably not such a good idea. Eventually I'd have to give her up, and I'm lousy at letting go."

"Maybe you wouldn't have to. Maybe *you* could adopt her."

"Me?" She shook her head. "Not without a father."

"Even if no one else was willing to take her? Minority children *are* sometimes difficult to place in adoptive homes. Besides, you never know," he said with a wink, "maybe a suitable father will come along."

Isabel issued an unladylike snort. "Yeah, right. I'm not holding my—"

At that moment, Craig Jaeger reappeared, bearing a steaming cup of coffee.

Dr. Keen gave Isabel a knowing look and another wink. "I believe I hear my pager," he said. "Oh, you can go up to the nursery and see the baby now, if you want." He quietly disappeared.

"Here," Craig said as he handed her the foam cup. "You look like you could use this."

What she could use was a bath, a comb, some decent clothes and maybe a little makeup. Until now she hadn't worried about her appearance. Suddenly she was acutely aware of the fact that she looked like someone's dirty laundry.

She took a grateful sip of the coffee. "Mmm, thank you. Doc said Sandy's doing just fine."

Craig almost smiled. "Good, good."

"Were you able to reschedule your meeting?"

"Unfortunately, no."

"I'm sorry. Hey, why don't you let me treat you to breakfast? It's the least I can do."

"Treat me with what? You aren't wearing a money belt under that sweatshirt, are you? Anyway, I thought you'd want to go up and see the baby."

She paused, willing the familiar ache in her heart to recede. He probably thought she was nuts, dismissing the child so quickly. But for her own good, she needed to avoid any further contact with Sandy. She became attached much too easily, then found it nearly impossible to let go. "If I go up to the nursery and press my nose against the glass, I might never leave," she said in a deliberately breezy tone. "But if you want to—"

"No," he said, shaking his head quickly. "I should get to the airport."

"Then you don't want breakfast?" The question came out sounding almost desperate. But she really needed an excuse to drag herself out of there before she became obsessed with that poor unwanted baby. Breakfast would do her good, especially breakfast with an obviously secure, seemingly compassionate and very sexy man. If anything could distract her from Sandy, Craig Jaeger could.

"Breakfast where?" he asked, wavering.

"Tito's Diner. My credit's good there—my parents own it."

After a little more arm-twisting he finally agreed, though he accepted with the enthusiasm he might reserve for an invitation to the guillotine.

His blue BMW still stood at the curb in front of the emergency room doors. No one had made a fuss about it being in the way on this slow morning. Craig scowled as he opened the passenger door.

Isabel slid in, the thrill of a challenge dulling the ache she felt at leaving Sandy behind. By the time breakfast was over, she vowed, she would win a smile from Craig Jaeger.

# Two

"Take a left at the next light," Isabel directed.

Why was he doing this? Craig wondered as he followed her instructions. Though it was impossible for him to make that meeting, he still needed to get to Dallas on the next available flight. If he hurried, he could still meet with most of the investors on an individual basis and reassure them that their money was being well spent.

Why, then, was Craig procrastinating? He looked over at Isabel. A melancholy sigh escaped her full lips as she closed her eyes in the face of the bright morning sun. He felt a primal tug deep inside. What man wouldn't choose Isabel's company over a string of stressful meetings?

"Turn right at the next corner," she said. "Then an immediate left into the driveway of the pink-and-lavender house."

"The pink-and-lavender...house," he repeated as he stared in awe at the impressive structure looming before him. It was three stories of Victorian excess, including a huge wraparound porch, towers and turrets, curlicues and froufrous, a slate roof and a weather vane. Ancient rosebushes, just starting to bloom in a pale pink, lined the wrought-iron fence that surrounded the property. "Is this where you live?"

She nodded. "And where I work. My business takes up most of the first floor." She nodded toward the demure, hand-painted shingle that hung on a post by the front steps: DeLeon Interiors.

They entered through a wide oak door with stained-glass panes. Inside, Craig found one of the most tastefully furnished offices he had ever seen, with fine old antiques, Oriental rugs, brass accents and thriving palms and ferns. Here and there were cozy seating arrangements with cushy-looking sofas and chairs and tables where, he imagined, clients could spread out samples and drawings or chat about their remodeling plans.

What struck Craig most forcefully, however, was that this place was an extension of Isabel herself—warm, caring and classy.

"I thought we were going to a diner," he said as she led him into a huge, ultramodern kitchen.

She grinned as she filled two mugs with coffee. "I changed my mind. My family is a nosy bunch. I started thinking about all the questions they would ask, and how they would make a fuss over what happened, so I decided a quiet breakfast here would be better. How do you take your coffee?"

"Black, thanks." He savored his first sip. The brew bore a touch of almond flavoring.

"Please, sit down," she said. "Be thinking about what you want to eat. Omelet, pancakes, waffles—I can do it all. I worked my way through college as a short-order cook at the diner. Meanwhile, I'm going to clean up a bit. Be back in about five minutes." She was briskly cheerful, but Craig sensed that she was forcing her mood. He suspected her thoughts were still with the baby.

As she left, she gave him an excellent view of her gently swaying hips. They were generous—not big, just more than a handful. In fact, although he couldn't tell exactly what was under the shapeless sweatshirt she wore, he got the distinct impression that *all* of Isabel was generous.

He had always liked a woman with some substance to her.

His body stirred slightly in a way that reminded him that he had gone a very long time without female companionship. Over the years he had learned that it took a surprising amount of effort to maintain an active social life, much less a real relationship, and his hectic work schedule simply didn't leave him enough time.

So what was he doing here, about to have an intimate breakfast with the saucy, sexy Isabel DeLeon?

When the swinging doors bounced open he expected Isabel to be returning. But although there was a definite family resemblance, the woman who entered the kitchen in a moth-eaten chenille robe was taller and thinner than Isabel. Her hair was lighter, too. And she carried a baby in her arms.

Isabel's sister and nephew, he presumed. The sleepy-eyed woman, who looked young enough to be in her teens, whisked right by him, oblivious to his presence, and headed for the coffeepot. It was only when Craig cleared his throat that she jumped and stared at him.

"Who are you?" she demanded as she clutched the baby protectively against her.

He stood and nodded politely toward the coffeepot, then poured a cup of coffee for her, since she obviously had her hands full. "Craig Jaeger. I'm a . . . friend of Isabel's. You're her sister?"

The woman nodded and relaxed a bit as she accepted the steaming mug, though the wariness remained in her eyes. "I'm Angie. Where's Isabel?"

"I'm here," interjected the melodious voice Craig was coming to enjoy. She entered the kitchen, her hair now loose and swept back from her face, falling in shimmering waves past her shoulders. "I see you two have met."

"Really, Iz," Angie said in a huff, "you could have warned me we had a guest." With that she made a dramatic exit, leaving a trail of coffee drips in her wake.

Isabel smiled apologetically. "She's a bear till she's had her morning dose of caffeine. So, what'll it be? How about eggs Benedict?"

"You have the stuff to make eggs Benedict?" His mouth watered at the thought.

"If you don't mind ham instead of Canadian bacon." Without delay she started the preparations.

Craig was fascinated by her competence. She made her own hollandaise sauce from scratch, for crying out loud. He was even more fascinated with her easy grace and the way the soft, faded fabric of her sweats molded to her voluptuous body whenever she reached for something.

"I'm impressed," he said.

"It's really easy."

An uncomfortable thought occurred to him. "Say, you don't have an irate husband who's going to wander in and hit the roof when he finds you cooking breakfast for a strange man, do you?"

She laughed, then sobered. "No. Not even a non-irate husband. In fact, it's a real treat to cook for someone besides myself and Angie."

"The treat is mine," he said, inhaling deeply of the toasted English muffins Isabel was buttering. "I tend to live on frozen dinners when I'm at home, and I'm at the mercy of strange restaurants when I travel."

"I take it that means you're not married." She placed the beautifully executed egg dish in front of him, along with a gravy boat of extra hollandaise sauce.

"No. I'm not the marrying kind, I'm afraid."

"Now, why do you say that?" she asked as she sat down with her own plate. "Did you have a bad experience with marriage?" She leaned slightly forward and cocked her head, as if listening intently. An impossibly light, floral scent teased him and then was gone.

She wasn't flirting, he decided, unsure if he was disappointed or not. Nor was she merely curious. She was actually concerned, and he decided her question deserved a serious answer. "I've never even tried. I work long hours and I travel, sometimes for weeks at a time. I couldn't manage that and a family, too."

He half expected her to object to his pat, well-rehearsed reply. Perhaps he even *wanted* her to say something about him needing to stop and smell the roses, or to suggest that a properly devoted wife would keep the home fires burning and support his career. But she did neither. Instead she merely looked down at her plate, her long, dark lashes casting exaggerated shadows against her cheeks.

He dug into his breakfast, finding the eggs perfectly poached, the ham tender, the muffin light and crispy. And if the breakfast was a treat for his taste buds, Isabel took care of his other senses. "This is wonderful," he said between bites.

"Thank you," she murmured. "I'll warm up the coffee."

He wasn't sure, but he got the distinct impression that he'd said something in the last few minutes that didn't sit well with his hostess.

Isabel refilled both cups and silently cursed her luck. He was handsome, successful, nice to talk to and quite possibly attracted to her—although she wasn't sure. But it didn't matter, because he was a confirmed bachelor. Or maybe he'd simply made that claim to curtail any designs she might have on his matrimonial status. Either way, he wasn't for her.

It wasn't that she was desperate to get married. But she had never felt comfortable dating a man when she knew the relationship wasn't headed somewhere. Sometimes she craved intimacy, but she couldn't see herself really close to a man without a serious commitment. So if there was no possibility of commitment, why bother?

Angie breezed back into the kitchen, thankfully interrupting the awkward silence. Nonetheless, Isabel stifled a groan when she noted her sister's getup. With her leather miniskirt, a clinging sweater and four-inch heels, she looked more like she was ready for a night at a disco rather than a day at work.

Angie wouldn't be interested in Craig. Her taste in men ran to destitute musicians, starving artists with long hair and earrings and the occasional student. But she obviously thought Craig was at least worth a flirtation.

"Hello," she said in the naturally husky voice Isabel had always envied. Angie looked right at Craig and batted her eyelashes. "I'm Angie, Isabel's sister, and I just came in here to let you know that that grouchy frump you saw earlier was my evil twin."

He smiled. Dammit, he actually smiled, and it was Angie who'd made him do it. "Pleased to meet you, Angie," he said, standing quickly, shaking her hand and then sitting back down.

Angie turned to Isabel. "Oh, Iz, don't forget your appointment with Mrs. Harrison at ten. I hope you aren't going to meet her like that!"

Isabel bit her lip. Angie's dig wasn't intentional. She wasn't malicious, just a bit self-possessed. "I thought I might take a shower and change clothes," Isabel responded mildly. "Where's Corey?"

"Oleta's visiting with him."

Again Isabel stifled the scolding she longed to give. She had told Angie over and over that Oleta, their housekeeper, was paid to clean, not baby-sit. But now wasn't the time to squabble.

"Well, see ya!" She breezed out, leaving a waft of expensive perfume behind her.

Craig arched his eyebrows as he watched her exit. "Quite a live wire, isn't she?"

"That's putting it mildly. She certainly keeps me on my toes."

He drained the last of his coffee. Isabel reached for the pot, but he shook his head. "I really have to go, and it sounds like you have things to do, too."

She couldn't deny it, although part of her wanted to drag out this pleasant interlude as long as possible. The man definitely did something to her blood pressure, and it wasn't just his looks or his self-confidence that attracted her, either. It was the concern he'd shown for Sandy that got to her. He'd turned something that most people would have considered a major annoyance into a personal responsibility. In a world where so few people were willing to take responsibility, his actions seemed particularly honorable, heroic, even.

Craig set his plate and cup in the sink, and then she walked him to the door. Naturally, Angie wasn't at her desk, yet, even though it was past eight-thirty. For once, Isabel was glad her sister was habitually late getting to work. She wanted some privacy during her last few moments with Craig.

He paused at the door. "I'd like to see you again, Isabel."

Although it was only a few minutes ago she'd been contemplating whether he felt the same attraction she did, she was actually surprised to have her suspicions confirmed. And she was tempted by his invitation. Oh, Lord, how she was tempted! The way he looked at her with those baby blues, waiting patiently for her to answer, made her insides melt.

But she knew what the answer had to be. They wanted different things out of life. If the two of them started dating, if they became involved, it would end in a mess with someone—most likely her—getting hurt.

"That's not a good idea," she said.

"Why not?"

*Why not?* "Well, I just don't think it would work out. Trust me, I'm not your type."

"Oh?" He leaned one of his muscular shoulders against the doorframe and crossed his arms. "And just who is 'my type'? Angie, maybe?"

Isabel shrugged uncomfortably. "The thought had crossed my mind. She made you smile."

As he straightened and moved closer, the look he gave her was deadly serious. "Your sister amuses me. You, on the other hand, interest me." His words sent a pleasurable chill up her spine. And when he touched her chin with just one finger, she thought her knees were going to give way. The kiss he bestowed on her was a mere brushing of lips, a mingling of breath before he pulled back.

"I . . . I did say no, didn't I?" she asked shakily.

Finally he smiled, just for her, and the effect was devastating. "You did. But I couldn't resist. Thanks for an interesting morning, Isabel. Goodbye." He turned and headed for his car. She stepped inside and closed the door before she did something dumb, like change her mind.

Isabel could easily have slipped to the floor in a puddle of pure goose bumps. That man was incredibly sexy. But there was the appointment with Mrs. Harrison to think about. Isabel would have to wait until later to fall apart.

She met her sister on the stairs. "Is he gone?" Angie asked excitedly.

"'Fraid so."

"Where did you find that guy, Iz? What's the story? And it's no wonder you never date—if you hang around good-looking, eligible men like *that!*"

"I didn't plan it," Isabel snapped. "Anyway," she couldn't resist adding, "*he* didn't think I looked so bad."

"Oooh!" Angie squealed. "Tell me, tell me."

"I have to get in the shower." Isabel resumed her trek upstairs, knowing full well Angie would drive herself crazy with her own curiosity. "I'll tell you later."

"Later" turned out to be lunchtime. The morning had been eaten up by meetings, deliveries, telephone emergencies and a pushy reporter from the *Galveston Free Press* who insisted on a lengthy interview with Isabel regarding the abandoned baby. Finally, after he'd been shooed away and Angie had taken time out to nurse Corey, Isabel was able to sit down with her sister, catch her breath and tell her about the morning's events.

"How sad," Angie said with a sob after she'd heard the whole story. She always got weepy when she nursed. "How could any mother abandon her own baby to die? I would have taken her. I would have nursed her right along with my own. I certainly have enough milk."

Isabel refrained from reminding her sister that immediately after Corey's birth, she had to be persuaded to even *touch* the baby—much less nurse him—she was so put out with all the trouble he'd caused. But the mother-child bond had become a strong one, once it had been established, Isabel now realized.

"Will Sandy be all right?" Angie asked.

"Dr. Keen thinks so."

Angie nodded with satisfaction, then smiled mischievously through her diminishing tears. "So what about Craig Jaeger?"

Isabel sighed glumly. "He asked me out."

"That's great! He's perfect for you—mature, stable-looking and he probably has a few bucks. When are you going out?"

"We're not. I turned him down."

Angie merely stared at her, stunned.

"He admitted that he's a workaholic, and he has no interest in marriage or family—ever." And in her present state of mind, after so recently holding the life of a newborn in her hands, she knew without a doubt that she wanted children.

"So? You couldn't even go out on one date? You're crazy, you know that? Completely crazy. What is this hang-up you have about marriage, anyway? And how do you know that he wouldn't fall in love with you and change his mind?"

"But what if I fell in love with him and he *didn't* change his mind?"

"So?" Angie said again. "You'd get over it! I hate to break this to you, Iz, but most guys don't ask a girl out planning to fall in love and marry her. It just happens, usually when they least expect it."

"And when did you become such an expert?"

Angie sighed. "I'm not, I guess, given this overwhelming evidence." She jiggled Corey and cooed at him, apparently not the least bit bitter about the way Corey's father had treated her.

Isabel managed to put Craig Jaeger and Sandy out of her mind a little while as she struggled through an afternoon every bit as hectic as the morning had been. But when Dr. Keen called her later that afternoon, everything else came to a screeching halt.

"Sandy's all right, isn't she?" Isabel immediately demanded.

"She's terrific. I don't plan to keep her here long."

"Has social services found a good foster home? I mean, they've been notified and all that, right?"

"Yes, Brenda Eams was here. You know her, I think."

"Oh, right, Brenda. She was Phil's caseworker." A tightness formed in her throat at the thought of Phil, her first and only foster child. He was back with his real mother, now, somewhere in Florida. She'd said good-bye to him three years ago, and she still missed him sometimes. "Brenda's good," she added. "I know she'll find just the right place for Sandy."

"Of course she will. She said she can always manage to wedge another little one in somewhere."

"What do you mean, 'wedge'?"

"It's just that all the available foster homes are packed right now. There's always a shortage. Well, there goes my page. I just wanted to let you know how—"

"Wait a minute. Did Brenda really think that placing Sandy would be a problem?"

"Nothing she can't handle. Sorry to run, Isabel, but—"

"I could take Sandy." The words came out of Isabel's mouth without any forethought.

"Oh, I certainly didn't mean to suggest—"

"That's exactly what you meant to suggest, and don't play innocent with me."

"Well, I *did* mention the possibility to Brenda. She said it would be no trouble to reactivate you as a foster parent. But don't feel like you have to—"

"I'll call her," Isabel said, her heart leaping in anticipation. "Oh, go answer your pager. You've done your job."

Minutes later, the deal was done. Brenda Eams had been ecstatic at the prospect of placing Sandy with Isabel. But Isabel hung up with mixed feelings. Part of her wanted to break into song and dance on her desktop. A baby of her own to care for! But the saner, more practical side of her knew how hard it would be to give Sandy up when the time came.

Well, there was no turning back now. She'd just signed up for a major heartbreak. But somehow she felt responsible to Sandy. She couldn't have said no to Dr. Keen's sly, backhanded request.

At four o'clock, she cornered Angie, who was in the workroom measuring fabric. "Can you hold down the fort for a while?"

"Sure. Where are you going?"

"To the hospital."

A wary look entered Angie's eyes. "Now, Iz, you aren't getting too attached to that baby, are you?"

Isabel nodded miserably. "'Fraid so. I agreed to foster her."

Angie exploded. "Are you actually suggesting we bring another newborn into this house? As if one isn't enough trouble!" She glanced over at the makeshift pallet on the floor, where Corey was sleeping peacefully. "We'll never get any work done," she added.

"As a matter of fact, one *isn't* enough trouble for two mothers, as you pointed out to me this morning. Besides, I think it'll work great. During the workday, we can share the child-care duties. And don't forget, at night you'll be taking yours home. Your *new* home."

"Oh, yeah. I forgot I was moving out." Angie's expression softened. "Do you really want a baby that badly?"

"Yes."

"You'll have to give her up eventually, you know."

"Maybe not. Dr. Keen thinks I should try to adopt her." Isabel hadn't realized she had taken his suggestion seriously until just now.

"Without a husband? I thought you didn't believe in raising a child without a father."

Isabel frowned. "I don't know. I'm still thinking."

"Well, I suppose two babies won't be *that* much more trouble than one," Angie said with a mischievous smile that belied her words.

Craig stared through the nursery window at the squirming infant. Once again, he asked himself, why? Why was he here? The small, wrapped gift he held in one hand was just an excuse, really.

The truth was, Sandy was his only remaining link with Isabel. That's why he was mooning over this baby.

He was still disappointed that Isabel had turned him down. He could have sworn he felt a spark between them during breakfast. And she certainly hadn't rejected his impulsive kiss. In fact, her reaction to his touch had been almost palpable. Why, then, had she refused to see him again?

A boyfriend, maybe. He'd asked her about a husband, but he hadn't brought up any other possibilities. It soothed his ego a bit to think that she'd rejected him not because she found him undesirable, but because her loyalties were committed elsewhere. It also made him outrageously jealous.

He tapped on the glass and made a funny face at the baby, although he knew she couldn't really see him. Nonetheless, she sort of smiled. Cute kid. He wondered what would become of her.

Gradually he became aware that he was no longer alone in the hospital corridor. He did a double take when he realized the woman approaching him was Isabel, conjured out of his dreams.

He wondered how much of his performance she had witnessed. He hadn't intended to be caught lurking here, making an ass of himself.

"Hello," Isabel said cordially as she drew closer to him. She wore tailored gray slacks and a pink silk blouse, allowing him to see more of the alluring shape he could only guess at before. "I thought you'd be in Dallas by now."

"Couldn't get a flight out," he said. "I'm going tomorrow, instead."

Lord, she was gorgeous, he thought, as every sensible word of conversation fled his suddenly fevered brain.

"Oh, look, there she is," Isabel said as she shifted her attention to the nursery. "Isn't she pretty?" Her tone was almost reverent.

"She looks like any other newborn," Craig groused, refusing to be drawn into some sentimental conversation.

"Excuse me, but that's my foster child you're maligning."

"You're taking her home?" he asked in surprise.

"There's a real shortage of foster homes right now. I sort of got drafted."

He wasn't sure why, but the knowledge that Isabel would be caring for Sandy eased his mind a lot. "I take it no one's come forward with information about her," he said, nodding toward Sandy.

Isabel shook her head. "It'll be on the news tonight and in tomorrow's paper. Maybe that will bring some results." She didn't sound overly thrilled by the prospect.

Craig was feeling more awkward by the moment. She hadn't asked him why he was here, as if it were perfectly natural for him to be goo-gooing at a baby that wasn't his, one he would probably never see again. He held the gift out. "Here, you open this."

She looked at the brightly wrapped package and then up at him, puzzled. "Excuse me?"

"It's a gift, for Sandy. I started thinking about her being here, no parents, and that maybe no one would give her any presents, and..." This explanation wasn't going the way he wanted it to. "Since you're going to be Sandy's temporary mom, you can open it."

"Oh, uh, okay."

Isabel's hands trembled as she meticulously unwrapped the package without tearing the paper. "Oh, this is lovely," she exclaimed as she examined the sterling-silver baby cup.

"I had it engraved with 'Sandy.' Do you think she'll get to keep that name?"

"I plan to call her Sandy for as long as I have her," Isabel said, her gaze still riveted on the cup as she turned it this way and that.

"And that's her birthstone," Craig explained when Isabel fingered the amethyst set in the cup below the name. "I just...I just wanted her to have something nice," he said lamely. Caught in the throes of a very unmanly emotion, Craig abruptly fled the scene.

Baffled, Isabel tucked the gift and its wrapping into her voluminous purse. For a man who claimed to never want children, he'd certainly been focused on Sandy when he thought no one was watching. His rapt attention to the child had brought a lump to her throat in addition to all the other myriad physical sensations his mere presence caused her.

Her pulse was still beating far above normal when a nurse poked her head out the nursery door. "Are you by any chance Isabel DeLeon?"

Isabel nodded.

"Aha. Dr. Keen said you would be by. You're going to be Sandy's foster-mother?"

"Yes, it looks that way."

"Would you like to hold her?"

"Oh, could I?"

"Sure." The nurse showed her into a small sitting room adjacent to the nursery. Moments later she brought a sleeping Sandy to Isabel, setting the tiny bundle into her arms.

A warm flood of maternal pride filled her, almost as if she'd borne the baby herself, instead of finding her on a beach. Oh, yes, adopting her was a definite possibility.

"She just ate," the nurse explained. "Has a real healthy appetite, that one does."

The nurse left them alone. Isabel leaned back in her chair, holding the baby in the crook of one arm. Then she pulled the silver cup from her purse with her free hand. "Look, Sandy," she crooned. "You have a present."

Sandy slept on.

Isabel took a closer look at the cup. It was heavy. Solid silver? she wondered. The amethyst looked like the real thing, too. She turned the cup over and read the inscribed words on the bottom: Jaeger Jewels.

Craig must be related somehow to that jewelry store in the historic district. The store was part of a chain. She remembered seeing one at the Galleria mall in Houston.

Gee, it would be nice to have a friend with jewelry business connections, she thought with a mischievous grin, especially one who was generous and good-looking enough to make a nun swoon. And judging from the way he was drooling in front of the nursery window, he wouldn't be a confirmed bachelor forever, no matter what he thought now. Was she nuts for letting him slip away?

Maybe she was, Isabel thought, reconsidering. The expression on his face as he had watched Sandy through the glass had said it all: he coveted this baby, whether he knew it or not.

She thought back to that moment in the emergency room, when he had touched Sandy's hand and then exchanged that potent, heated glance with Isabel. Could a bond really form that quickly?

Hugging Sandy to her, feeling a oneness of spirit with her, Isabel acknowledged that a bond could form instantly—for her, anyway. But she really didn't have time to worry about Craig's bond, if it even existed. The next few days would be devoted to preparing her home for Sandy's arrival. She would have to buy a crib and clothes and toys and diapers and...

Suddenly she felt mean-spirited to exclude Craig. His part in saving Sandy's life had been every bit as crucial as hers. Maybe she should call him and offer him the chance to spend time with Sandy, if he wanted. Yes, that would ease her conscience.

# Three

Craig didn't know quite what to make of it when Isabel called him at the Blue Waters construction office a few days later with a rather nervously worded invitation.

"...and I thought you might want to come shopping with me," she said. "I need to pick out some baby things for Sandy, you know, a crib and clothes and toys and things."

Shopping? She had to be kidding. He couldn't see himself picking out teddy bears and frilly little dresses. Apparently she had gotten the wrong idea about him from his admittedly bizarre behavior at the hospital.

"It's not that I wouldn't like to see you," he said carefully, "but I had in mind a candlelight dinner for two."

"Oh." There was a long pause. "Well, see, I was

afraid you were feeling left out about Sandy," she said in a small voice.

No way! Well, he *had* been thinking about Sandy and Isabel more than was normal, wondering how they were getting along. But he was sure it was only a temporary fascination, one that would pass of its own accord if he left it alone. "I was just worried about the kid's welfare. But now that I know she's receiving adequate care…" God, he sounded cold. "She's doing okay, isn't she? Eating well and all that?"

"Oh, yes, she's wonderful. In fact, she's right here in my lap, fast asleep."

The picture that flashed into his mind made his breath catch in his throat. "That's good," he muttered.

"But you don't want to go shopping with me."

"Isabel, I'd go anywhere with you. Just so you understand that my motives have nothing to do with the baby." That, at least, was true. He would be interested in Isabel, baby or no.

Another long pause. She was probably trying to decide whether to quickly close this can of worms … or give him a chance. "What time would you like to go?" she finally asked. "The mall is open late tonight."

"I could pick you up after work and take you to dinner," he suggested. "Then we could take care of the shopping, and maybe go to a movie."

"I can't do all that, not with a little baby!" Her objection was immediate and strenuous. "Sandy's only a few days old. Look, let's forget the shopping. It was a dumb idea, anyway. In a couple of weeks things will settle down, and I'll feel more comfortable leaving the baby for a few hours. We could go out then, if you want."

He did want—very much. "Great," he agreed before she could change her mind. "I'll call you in a couple of weeks, then." But as she gave him her phone number, he had this nagging feeling that he'd blown it by not jumping at the chance to shop for baby clothes.

At the other end of the line, Isabel quietly hung up the phone and pondered Craig's reaction. It might be that he was deliberately denying his attachment to Sandy, perhaps distrustful of new, alien feelings. Or maybe, she acknowledged wryly, his interest in the baby was no more than a Good Samaritan's concern, and she was wrongly interpreting his actions to fit in with this bonding theory of hers.

There was only one way to find out, and that was to get to know him better. If, after she did, she figured out that he really wasn't good father material, as he claimed, she would break things off neatly, cleanly— before either one of them got too involved.

That was the plan, at least. But she had this niggling suspicion that if she let him kiss her again, all bets were off.

On a Saturday morning two weeks later, Isabel entertained a freshly bathed Sandy with a monologue while she put on a fresh diaper. "It was nice of you to let your mom sleep in this morning, yes it was," she cooed. Publicly she called herself the baby's "Aunt Izzy," but in private she thought of herself as a mommy. She certainly felt like one.

Someday she might actually *be* Sandy's mother, she mused happily, fastening the last snap on the baby's romper. She had an appointment scheduled for Monday with Social Services to formally apply for Sandy's

adoption. The prospect filled her with hope and opti-
mism.

She felt a stab of worry at the thought of leaving
Sandy tonight. Craig had called, as promised, and in-
vited her out for a dinner at a classy ocean-side restaurant. Angie had volunteered to bring Corey over and
stay with both babies. So why was Isabel worried?

Maybe it wasn't worry, but guilt. She'd spent every
waking moment and many sleeping ones with Sandy
ever since she'd taken her home from the hospital. She
was actually looking forward to leaving the baby behind for a few hours. She was really looking forward to
spending those few hours with Craig Jaeger.

She could handle it, she told herself. There was no
law that said she had to fall in love with the guy. If a
ready-made family wasn't on his agenda, she could still
enjoy just being with him. Angie had told her so.

And Angie knew so much about relationships.

The rest of the morning was a frenzy of feeding,
playing and rocking as Isabel tried to get in a whole
day's worth of mothering in just a few hours. In the afternoon, as Sandy slept, Isabel pampered herself with
a manicure and facial. Ordinarily she went to a salon for
those services, but having a baby had tied her down
considerably.

She didn't mind.

Somehow she managed to dress and do her hair and
makeup between feeding and diapers and baby laundry. She was ready by the time Angie showed up, dragging a diaper bag in one hand and Corey tucked under
the other arm, as if she'd been hauling kids around her
whole life.

"You didn't have to bring diapers," Isabel chided, resisting the urge to take Corey and cuddle him. She could just imagine what baby drool would do to silk.

"Yes I did. Corey has special *boy* diapers. They make different kinds, you know." Angie spoke with the authority of Dr. Spock. "Hey, you look spiffy. That's a new outfit. When can I borrow it?"

Isabel straightened the collar of the cream silk jumpsuit. "It wouldn't be long enough for your racehorse legs."

"So, I'll tuck the pants into boots or something. Where's the peanut?"

"Upstairs asleep. I really should wake her or she'll be up all night." She headed for the stairs.

Angie halted her sister with a tug to her arm. "I'll take care of it. You have pressing business elsewhere. I think I hear Craig's Beamer out front."

Isabel found herself hyperventilating. This is ridiculous, she told herself. Craig Jaeger was just a man, a man she probably wouldn't be seeing again after tonight. They would discover they had nothing in common, and that would be the end of it.

And what about this bonding business? a small voice asked.

Wishful thinking, that was all. Craig had said he wasn't interested in the baby beyond a humanitarian concern, and she had no real reason to disbelieve him.

"Aren't you going to get the door?" Angie asked.

"Oh, yeah." She started for the front door when an impatient squall from upstairs stopped her. She stood indecisively in the entry hall, wanting to move in two directions at once.

"Get the door!" Angie said as she strapped Corey into his little chair. "I'll take care of Sandy."

Already feeling like a neglectful mother, Isabel opened the door. All thoughts of Sandy immediately fled her mind as she took in the sight of Craig Jaeger standing on her front porch. Gone was the somber business suit she'd seen him wear before, replaced by dark olive slacks that accentuated his lean hips, a grey-green Oxford shirt—obviously tailored to fit his wide shoulders—and a tie that was a bold splash of color.

But it was the look in his eyes that stole her breath away. There was a certain devilish sparkle in their blue depths that warned her she was in over her head.

"You're beautiful," he said with a crooked smile, revealing a flash of white teeth.

Whatever she'd been about to say in response stuck in her throat when Sandy let out another irritated shriek.

"Good grief, is that Sandy?"

Isabel looked over her shoulder, wondering what the problem was. "Uh-huh. Would you like to see her?" she asked hopefully.

He hesitated, his gaze flickering toward the stair-case. "Ah, no. That is, I'd love to, but our reservations are for eight."

"Oh, right. Let me just check—"

"Would you go, already?" Angie interrupted as she came down the stairs carrying the screaming infant. "She's just hungry, that's all."

"But—" Isabel protested.

"Come along, little mother," Craig cajoled, taking her hand and guiding her out the door. He looked over his shoulder, though, a slight wrinkle to his brow. "Looks like Sandy's in competent hands."

Isabel barely managed to grab her purse, still calling last-minute instructions as Craig closed the door behind her.

"I'm sorry," she said when they were in the car and safely away from the house. "I've never left her before. And the way she was crying . . . she doesn't usually cry like that."

"No? I thought babies cried all the time."

"Not Sandy. Oh, when she's wet or hungry she'll boohoo a little, but not that all-out, red-in-the-face squalling. I hope she's okay."

"I'm sure she's fine. What do you do with her when you're working?"

"Sandy and Corey share a crib in the back room. Angie and I take turns with diaper and bottle duty. It works out fine for now, but when they start sleeping less and crawling and whatnot, I plan to hire a nanny. That way we can keep the babies close by but still be able to work."

"Sounds like a good arrangement."

When they arrived at the restaurant, the first thing Isabel did was head for the pay phone.

Craig grabbed her hand before she could insert the quarter. "We just left them ten minutes ago."

"I know. But I forgot to tell Angie to—"

"Relax, Isabel. Everything will be fine. Angie has the number for the restaurant, right?"

Isabel sighed. "You're right. I'm being ridiculous."

She tried to enjoy the excellent prime rib, but her thoughts kept drifting. She realized halfway through dinner that she'd done nothing but talk about Sandy from the moment Craig had arrived at her door.

"I'm really sorry," she said after stopping herself in the middle of a long diatribe about boy diapers and girl diapers. "I've always despised new mothers and their dreary talk of teething and colic, and here I am inflicting the same silly stuff on an innocent victim. And you don't even *like* babies."

"I never said I didn't *like* babies," he huffed.

"Well, no, but—"

"I do like them. Honestly. I mean, I don't *dis*like them."

"But you don't want to be a father."

"Not because I don't like children. I just don't think it would be fair to inflict my parenting instincts on any kid." His words were light, but there was something beneath his glibness, something that caused his brow to tighten and his lips to firm.

"You aren't born with parenting instincts. It's something that just sort of grows on you. Part of the bonding process," she ventured, thinking of Angie.

Craig looked away pointedly, then flagged their waiter. "Would you like dessert? They have a wonderful black-bottom pie here."

Well, what had she expected? She must be nuts, grilling him about his decision to remain a bachelor.

She seriously considered dessert, but the sleek jumpsuit was feeling a bit snug after the sumptuous dinner, so she declined. "What I need is a nice, brisk walk."

"Great idea." Craig quickly paid the check, and before she realized where her innocent suggestion would take them, he had led her outside and onto a deserted, moonlit beach.

"Hey, I just realized we're not too far from where I found San—" She cut herself off. Damn, she was doing it again. She wished her guardian angel would pinch her and make her shut up. She was an intelligent woman, a college graduate with a challenging career.

Surely she could dredge up some topic of conversation that would be interesting to both of them.

"I'm sorry," she said once again, then gave an embarrassed laugh. "I admit it—I'm obsessed. I was like that with my first foster child, too. I'll get over it."

"I didn't realize you'd been a foster-mother before," he said, taking her hand in a perfectly natural gesture as they started walking along the hard-packed sand. "When was that?"

"I'll tell you about it another time, maybe." Talking about Phil still had the capacity to choke her up sometimes. "You've probably had just about enough kidtalk for one evening. I . . . I really wanted tonight to be different," she said on a sigh. "I wanted you to see that I could be . . ." She shrugged. "I'm not at my best."

"Then your best must be pretty spectacular."

The low timbre of his voice sent a pleasurable shiver up her spine, one she was sure he noticed.

They paused to look out over the gently rolling waves gilded with moonlight. He stood behind her, his hands resting on her shoulders. She could feel the vitality of his body, the warmth of his breath stirring her hair.

Slowly he swiveled her around until she faced him, and he was closer still. "Isabel, you might not believe this, but I don't really mind your talking about Sandy. Your eyes light up and you smile a lot and you get very animated. I find it extremely attractive. There's nothing sexier than a woman who's excited about something."

*Sexy?* She closed her eyes. "You don't have to say that just to make me feel—"

"Hush." In the next second his mouth descended on hers. This kiss was neither tender nor tentative, as the first one had been. It was a kiss of hunger, of possession and of raw, barely controlled passion.

And suddenly she couldn't get enough of it. She leaned into him, wrapping her arms around his neck, pressing the length of herself against him and opened her mouth to his sensual assault. His powerful aura enveloped her like a welcoming cocoon. She buried her hands in his thick, black hair, pulling him closer still.

As his mouth left hers to explore the curve of her neck, his hands burned trails of fire down her back and smoothed the soft silk against her skin and along her hips. A coil of heat took shape deep in her chest, then moved lower, causing her stomach to tighten. When he reached lower to lightly cup her bottom, her every muscle tensed with the startling pleasure of his touch.

Nothing like this had ever happened to Isabel. She wasn't unfamiliar with desire. She had experienced moments of passion and the satisfaction of needs. But never this . . . this white-hot yearning to be close, to be as one.

Surprisingly, the drive had every bit as much to do with her heart as it did her flesh. She felt something for this man, whose hands were strong enough to crush bricks, she imagined, yet so gentle when he wanted to be. She would never forget the expression on his face when he'd gazed at Sandy through the hospital nursery window.

A rush of affection welled up inside her, and she grasped his smoothly shaven face between her palms and pressed her lips to his again.

Craig groaned as his tongue dueled with hers and his hands, so warm, roved over her back, making her wish he could reach her bare skin.

Some small grain of self-preservation warned her that things could quickly get out of control. She paused to draw in a ragged breath, brushing her cheek against his as her heart pounded in her ears.

He slowly withdrew, showing more control than she did. But she couldn't help feeling slightly relieved. The panicky thrill that had filled her receded as he downgraded the passionate kiss to a warm hug. Still, her knees trembled and her stomach was full of frenetic butterflies.

Lord, just because a lethally sexy man had kissed the stuffing out of her, it was no reason to go to pieces.

He pulled away from her, making sure she was steady on her feet before letting go. She was glad he did, because she was downright shaky. Falling on her face would not add to her already unchic image.

"That was interesting," he said.

"Yes." Understatement of the year.

"Got a little carried away."

"Mmm," she said noncommittally. She didn't want to be too complacent, as if such lusty encounters were commonplace with her, but neither did she want to complain about it. "Unusual, but it sure beat the dessert we passed up."

He smiled, and the tension between them began to abate. "We should probably go. I know you're anxious to get home."

She was, and yet she wasn't. Of course she missed the baby, but she was reluctant to say good-night to Craig. He was the most intriguing man...but how did she know that? She'd been so busy talking babies, she'd hardly let him get a word in edgewise. He probably had a million fascinating stories. She hadn't even asked him about his condominium project, or his relation to Jaeger Jewels, and he'd volunteered very little.

On the short drive home, she fought the urge to ask him if he wanted to see her again. She waited, hoping he would bring up the subject, but he remained maddeningly quiet.

He pulled his BMW up to the curb in front of her house. "Who's that in your driveway?" he asked.

"What?" She'd been so preoccupied, she hadn't noticed the Mercedes station wagon illuminated by Craig's headlights. She recognized it immediately, and panic welled up inside her like a volcanic eruption. "Oh, my God, that's Dr. Keen's car!" she cried, lunging for the door handle.

She was out of the car and running across the front yard so fast, Craig had a hard time catching up with her. Dr. Keen, he remembered with a wave of foreboding, was that pediatrician from the hospital.

By the time Isabel worked her key into the front-door lock and pushed it open, Craig was right behind her, his insides frozen with fear. God in heaven, what was wrong? If there'd been an accident or serious illness, wouldn't Angie have called an ambulance?

The sound of babies crying was plainly audible the moment they were inside. That was a good sign, Craig decided. Both children were alive and breathing, at least. Isabel, though, gave a little gasp of terror as she headed for the stairs, then bounded up them two at a time.

He followed her into the nursery, immediately taking in the picture and realizing that nothing was seriously wrong. The white-haired doctor sat in a rocking chair, rubbing one baby's tummy, while Angie was putting the other in a swing.

The nursery, like the rest of the house, was tastefully decorated to the hilt. There were no loud cartoon characters or clowns or balloons for Sandy, just soft blues and yellows in muted prints that were a soothing counterpoint to the wailing. How could two such tiny human beings make so much noise?

Make that three human beings, one not quite so tiny. Angie was sobbing uncontrollably, too. "Oh, Isabel, I'm so glad you're home!" she cried, throwing her arms around her big sister.

"What's going on?" Isabel demanded, extricating herself from Angie's tenacious grasp and reaching for the baby Dr. Keen held, which Craig presumed was Sandy.

"Just a touch of colic, nothing to worry about," the doctor replied, placing Sandy in Isabel's waiting arms.

Isabel paced and cooed and jiggled and patted in an effort to comfort, but she had no better luck than Dr. Keen. The squalling continued. She turned accusing eyes on her sister. "Why didn't you call me?"

Angie dissolved into tears once again. "I thought I could handle it. Besides, I didn't want to interrupt the first date you've had in two years...." Her hand flew to her mouth as her gaze darted to Craig, who stood just inside the nursery door.

Isabel bit her lip and said nothing, although her face turned a becoming shade of pink. Craig was inordinately pleased to know that Isabel was choosy about whom she went out with.

"I called Dr. Keen just to ask for advice," Angie continued.

"And I volunteered to come over and help out." Dr. Keen supplied the answer. "As a family friend, not as a physician. Angie did the right thing, Isabel. There was no need to cut short your evening. You couldn't have done anything, anyway. There's not much you can do for a colicky baby."

Isabel looked only slightly mollified.

Dr. Keen gave an elaborate yawn. "Well, I think things are pretty well under control now," he said, despite the fact that Sandy was still crying. Corey, at least, had quieted. Dr. Keen held out his hand to Craig, and the two men reintroduced themselves. "I'll show myself out," the doctor said, slipping from the room.

"Maybe I should make you two a pot of coffee," Craig offered with a wry smile. "Looks like you might be up for a while."

The last thing Isabel wanted was for Craig to be further exposed to two squalling babies and two slightly crazed moms tearing their hair out, not to mention a messy house that smelled overwhelmingly like pine disinfectant. He would forever rule out family life.

"That's okay," she said, edging him out the nursery door toward the stairs. "I'm sure things will settle down soon."

Craig knew how to take a hint. Isabel was politely giving him the boot. Still, he paused to study the baby in her arms and got his first close-up look at Sandy since the day of her birth.

"She looks different," he observed.

"At this age, they change almost daily. Do you...do you want to hold her?"

He'd just as soon not. Frankly, he was numbed by the mere thought of holding something so small and fragile. He remembered feeling that way about his little brother, Tom, when he'd come home from the hospital. Craig had been only ten years old, and he'd been scared to death at the prospect of holding a six-pound infant. But before long, the terror he'd felt had been replaced by an awesome sense of responsibility. With his mother dead and his father gone away so often on business, Tom had no family to rely on except Craig.

"Craig?"

This was different, he told himself. Besides, he felt compelled to defend his statement about disliking babies. "Sure, I'll hold her, but maybe I'd better sit down." He perched on the top step and warily accepted the red-faced little bundle, settling her against his shoulder, where she could scream in his ear.

He patted her back and rocked her back and forth. To his utter amazement, within less than a minute her cries diminished.

"Would you look at that?" Angie observed from the nursery doorway. "The kid's been crying for hours on end. How'd you do that?"

"Beginner's luck, I guess." He tried not to let on, but he felt a tremendous sense of satisfaction at being the one to make Sandy stop crying.

Isabel sat down on the step next to him. "I'll take her back now, if you'd like."

"Oh, sure, now that she's quiet," he teased, but he handed over the drowsy infant with undeniable relief.

As he watched Isabel, her attention focused totally on Sandy, he could hardly believe the effect she had on him. With her compassion and her dark, sultry eyes and her sweet, musical voice, she was just about the most enchanting creature Craig had ever seen. Not the most glamorous woman at the moment, perhaps, with talcum powder on her nose and her hair escaping from its pins into untidy tendrils, but she was definitely enchanting.

When she sang a few lines from a Spanish lullaby to Sandy, he went all mushy inside.

He had to get out of there. This sort of thinking was dangerous to a confirmed bachelor like him. He had no business getting this close to her or the kid...*especially* the kid. Neither of them had said anything about seeing each other again, and he didn't plan to mention it. He wanted Isabel with a desire so sharp he could taste it. But she had needs, too, and they involved a lot more than pleasures of the body.

He couldn't give her what she needed.

"I'd better be going," he said with a deceptively casual tone. "Don't get up. I wouldn't want you to wake Sandy. I can see myself out."

"Thank you for dinner," she said. "It was marvelous. I just hope I didn't bore you to tears."

"I wasn't bored." Honestly, he hadn't been. He had thoroughly enjoyed hearing all about Sandy. That's what worried him. He leaned over and gave Isabel an altogether proper kiss on the cheek, but he was thinking about that *im*proper kiss on the beach. It was probably a good thing she was holding a baby and her sister was only a few short steps away, or he would be tempted to take another sample of Isabel's sweet, hot passion.

He lightly touched Sandy's fuzzy head and gave them both a parting smile before descending the stairs and letting himself out into the cool night air. Surely that ache in his chest wasn't loneliness.

Two days later, Isabel sat in one of those nondescript, cheaply furnished government offices, filling out all the appropriate forms of application to adopt Sandy. Brenda Eams, Sandy's social worker, was helping.

"An abandoned child has to remain a ward of the state for at least a year," she explained, "to be absolutely sure the parents can't be found. But after that, Sandy will be up for grabs."

"Do you think I'll have much trouble?" Isabel asked, rubbing the tense muscles at the back of her neck. The application process had been quite an ordeal. "Sandy is definitely Hispanic—it's becoming more apparent every day."

"Well, it's true that minority babies aren't in as much demand as Anglo children are," Brenda said. "And since you're Sandy's foster-mother, that would give you an edge—provided everything goes okay for the next year."

Isabel nodded eagerly.

"However..." Brenda worried her lower lip with her teeth.

Isabel's heart sank. "What?"

"There is a young Hispanic couple on the waiting list. They've been waiting for a baby girl, and I think they would jump at the chance to adopt Sandy."

"But I'm Hispanic, too," Isabel argued. "Well, half, anyway." Her mother was as Irish as a shamrock, although none of her children had inherited her red hair and fair skin.

"That's not the problem. But I'm afraid your, er, marital status is." Brenda dropped her head, embarrassed.

"But lots of single parents adopt children. I thought the state didn't have a problem with that anymore."

"They don't, not too much, but the preference is still for two parents. All I'm saying is that it's not guaranteed you'll get Sandy. Now if you were to get married, you'd be a shoo-in! I don't suppose you have any plans in that direction, do you?''

"Well, er, no, not exactly." Craig Jaeger's roguish face popped into her mind. Rather than quickly dismiss him, as she knew she should, she continued to hold him in her thoughts; and a chill, the kind she got when she *knew* she was onto something important, shot up her spine and down her arms.

This was dangerous territory, she told herself. Before, she'd been thinking in the abstract, hoping that Craig would *someday* see himself as a husband and father, so that *maybe*, if they fell in love, they would have a future together. Now her fantasies were taking a rather specific turn.

"There *is* someone," Brenda said in a low, conspiratorial voice. "Can you rope him in?"

Isabel smiled sadly and shook her head. She'd been on one rather disastrous date with this guy, and she was still thinking of him as husband material? She must be loco. Besides, Craig would never be "roped in" to something he was dead set against, no matter how strong the sexual attraction between them.

If she so much as mentioned marriage, he would probably think she was a lunatic and head for the hills.

Maybe in time a close relationship would develop between them, and Craig would realize on his own that fatherhood was exactly what he needed in his life. In time. But how much time did she have?

# Four

---

Craig didn't know where he was going, only that he needed to get away from the Blue Waters construction site. Sometimes being in the middle of things, watching his ideas take shape, gave him a feeling of accomplishment. Other times—like tonight—it reminded him that he'd let his old man manipulate him.

Still wearing the jeans and work shirt he favored for his on-site work, Craig climbed into his BMW and headed out in no particular direction with all the windows open. He hoped the salt breeze would wash the stress right off him. But his troubling thoughts about his father continued to plague him.

Sinclair Jaeger, an international gem dealer, and later head of a multimillion-dollar empire, had spent most of his adult life pretending he didn't have children. Now suddenly Sinclair was having second thoughts about the sons he'd neglected. It was too late for Tom, but over the past year or so he'd tried to draw Craig into one business venture after another—business being the only arena in which Sinclair could relate to anyone.

Craig had resisted. His father's efforts were too little, too late. But Sinclair wasn't a man to give up when he wanted something. Craig had been flabbergasted to learn that the cartel of developers who'd hired his small construction firm to build Blue Waters was headed by none other than Sinclair Jaeger.

Craig had been forced to do business with his father or lose the job, and there were too many people depending on Blue Waters for him to chuck it. But he kept his personal dealings with Sinclair to a minimum, much to his father's irritation.

The farther Craig got from Blue Waters, the better he felt—until he realized where he'd been unconsciously heading. He touched the brake, slowing down so he could fully appreciate the sight of the huge, icing-sugar house, wanting to stop, knowing he shouldn't.

It had been three weeks since his date with Isabel. In that time, he'd picked up the phone a dozen times intending to call her, and always he managed to talk himself out of it.

He slowed the car to a crawl, then pulled up to the curb. It wouldn't hurt if he just stopped in to say hi and ask how Sandy was doing, he thought as he climbed out of the car, his heart a little lighter. But no one answered the doorbell. His disappointment weighed him down again, even as he told himself it was for the best if he didn't see her.

He drove aimlessly through town, getting caught up in cars and tourist traffic around the Strand, the city's historic business district, and not really caring about the delay. He was surrounded by carefree people enjoying the warm summer weather—parents with children, honeymooning couples—which only added to his isolation.

He'd been working almost round-the-clock since moving down here from Dallas to oversee Blue Waters, so he hadn't had time to make many friends. In fact, Isabel was one of the few people he'd met outside the construction business, and he'd deliberately neglected that association.

He supposed he deserved to be lonely.

He was just about to head back to the construction trailer, his temporary quarters until the first model condominium was completed, when a neon sign caught his eye: Tito's Diner.

It was the diner Isabel's family owned, he realized even as he turned the steering wheel, guiding the car into the crowded parking lot. He wasn't sure why he was doing this: maybe, unable to touch Isabel, he wanted to touch something that was close to her. Or maybe he simply didn't want to be by himself.

The restaurant, off the beaten path and not in a terribly fashionable district, wasn't the sort of place Craig usually frequented. With his architect's eye, he placed the construction in the 1950s, a little worn at the heels but not shabby. Once inside, he could see that the clientele was mixed—some families, some blue-collar workers, a few more upscale yuppie types. No tourists.

An attractive older woman with flaming red hair stood behind the cash register counting out change to a customer. As she counted, her blue-eyed gaze met Craig's. "You can have a seat anywhere you can find one, sugar. Specials are up on the chalkboard."

Craig nodded, inwardly smiling at the idea of anyone calling him "sugar." He wandered into the dining room and found an empty stool at the counter. He liked this place, he decided. It had a warm, comfortable feeling about it, and the food smelled great.

A waitress set a glass of ice water and a menu in front of him. "Hi, can I get you something to—Craig?"

"Isabel?" Craig said at the same time. It had taken him a moment to realize that the curvaceous package standing behind the counter in jeans and a blue-and-white "Tito's" apron was none other than Isabel herself. "I knew your parents owned this place, but what are you doing here?"

"I fill in occasionally when someone's sick or on vacation." After her initial surprised outburst, her voice had cooled considerably. He couldn't blame her. She probably thought he hadn't called her because he hadn't enjoyed her company, which couldn't be further from the truth.

"Where's Sandy?" he asked.

"Nanno, my grandmother, is taking care of her. She has a little apartment in back of the restaurant."

"Hey, lady," a man at the end of the counter called out, "what do I have to do to get a coffee refill?"

Isabel pasted on a smile. "Coming right up." She turned away from Craig to take care of business. So he figured if he wanted any attention from her he'd better order some food.

"So what's good?" he asked when she returned, order pad and pen in hand.

"Everything. Papa wouldn't put it on the menu if it wasn't good."

"But you must have a favorite."

She sighed. "If you like Mexican, the enchilada dinner. For American food, try the pork tenderloin," she said dutifully.

"Okay, I'd like the enchilada dinner, ice tea . . . and how about a small break?"

"What would you like broken?" she asked sweetly.

"Ah, c'mon, Isabel."

"Hey, miss," the persistent customer at the end of the counter called out again. "Where's my meat loaf?"

She gave a helpless shrug and waltzed away. Craig got the distinct impression she enjoyed giving him the cold shoulder. She really was busy, so he didn't bother her. But he did watch her as she bustled around, a coffeepot in one hand, stacks of dishes in the other and a dish towel slung over one shoulder. She laughed and bantered with the other customers, many of whom were apparently regulars, and she deftly parried several flirtations.

More than once her gaze collided with his, and the smile fled from her face to be replaced by a perplexed frown.

Craig was fascinated with the family dynamics going on in the kitchen, too, which was open to his full view. The older Hispanic man who presided over the ancient grill had to be Isabel's father. Two younger men, who with their dark, curly hair were almost identical, were obviously Isabel's brothers. Craig would have noted the family resemblance even without the teasing and grousing that advertised the fact they were all siblings. And the woman with the red hair behind the cash register would be Isabel's mother. Her coloring contrasted sharply with the others in the DeLeon family, but she and Isabel both shared that cute little ski-slope nose.

Although the elder DeLeon yelled a lot and brandished his spatula like an avenging sword, he smiled a lot, too. The two brothers argued good-naturedly; any fool could see how strong the familial bonds were. And

Isabel—she positively basked in the glow of her family, even when she was barking back a smart retort or popping one of them with her dish towel.

Craig felt an unexpected tightness in his chest, a feeling he could almost identify as jealousy. He'd grown up with every advantage money could buy, but he'd never experienced the closeness of family, even before his mother had died. Both of his parents had spent more time jetting from one exotic locale to another than they had with their kids.

Craig had tried to make up for his father's absence—God, how he'd tried to be a good big brother to Tom. But he could count on one hand the number of times he and Tom had shared a good laugh, or a hug, or even a healthy argument. He didn't need *any* hands to count the number of such moments with his father.

A steaming plate of enchiladas, Spanish rice and refried beans appeared before Craig. The scent made his mouth water.

"Can I get you anything else?" Isabel asked.

Craig looked up. He could tell she was itching to get away from him. "Yeah, how about five minutes of your time? I'd like to explain—"

"Craig, you don't owe me anything," she said, pressing her hands against the counter and looking anywhere but at him. "We went on one date. So, it didn't work out. I had no right to be snippy with you."

"Maybe not *snippy*," he said, amused by the aptly descriptive word, "but you had a right to be a little confused. We had a wonderful evening, and I never followed up."

She checked her watch, biting her lip indecisively. "I go on break in a few minutes. We can talk then." She didn't appear terribly thrilled at the prospect, but he'd take what he could get.

The enchiladas were fantastic. Or maybe it was the anticipation Craig felt that only made the food seem to taste better. He relished every bite and was even pondering a selection of homemade pies for dessert when he felt, rather than saw, Isabel's presence behind him. She set a cup of black coffee on the counter, then slid onto the stool next to his.

When he looked at her, he noticed that she'd removed her apron, combed her hair and put on fresh lipstick. Not that she needed to do any of that for him— he thought she was gorgeous no matter what—but the fact that she'd taken the trouble pleased him no end.

"The banana-cream pie is the best on this planet," she said. "It's Nanno's specialty."

Suddenly he was less interested in pie than he'd been moments earlier. He was craving the sweeter taste of Isabel's lips, so moist and pink. The craving was all the sharper because he already knew how she tasted, how her soft, expressive mouth would feel against his.

"Craig?"

"I'd better pass," he said, patting his flat stomach.

"Worried about your weight?" she said with a skeptical tilt of her head. "If you're into health food, this is the wrong restaurant."

"I didn't come here for the food."

"Then why are you here?" she asked, her brown eyes snapping with challenge.

"I'm not sure. I stopped at your house, but no one was home. Then I passed this place, and I remembered your family owned it. Is Tito your father?"

"Tito was the previous owner. When Papa bought the diner, he couldn't afford to change the sign. Then, when he *could* afford it, he figured, why tamper with success?''

Craig nodded. ''Makes sense. It's nice that you help out here. I doubt you need the money.''

''Do you, now?''

''I asked around about you. You're very well respected in this city. In fact, I was thinking of asking you to put in a bid on decorating the models at Blue Waters.''

''So this is a business call?'' she asked. He thought she looked disappointed. Or maybe that was just wishful thinking on his part.

''No. In fact, we can talk about that some other time. I really wanted to see you. Personally.''

She made no response to that, except to take a sip of her coffee.

''I had a great time when we went out.''

''I enjoyed it, too,'' she said cautiously. Her tennis shoe, resting on the footrail of her stool, wiggled out a silent but frantic rhythm. ''Would you mind if we walked outside? I could use some fresh air.'' Without waiting for his consent, she slid off her stool and led the way to the exit. Mrs. DeLeon stared at them curiously as they passed her at the cash register.

Isabel didn't stop until she'd led Craig through the parking lot and around to the side of the building, where a pleasant plot of green grass shaded by two palm trees was tucked away from public view. She walked toward a stone bench that separated the two trees, but she seemed too agitated to sit down.

Craig took her hand and drew her down on the bench beside him. He kept hold of her hand, just in case she had any ideas about running away. ''I want to see you again,'' he said point-blank.

Her eyes widened slightly. "But?"

"Why are you so sure there's a 'but'?"

"It's taken you three weeks to decide this. Something was holding you back."

He didn't jump to deny it. "I admit, I've had to sort a few things out. In fact, I'm not sure they're all sorted, yet."

"What kinds of things?"

"Like where I could possibly fit into your life. You've just taken on an enormous responsibility with Sandy."

"That's true. She does take an incredible amount of time. But that doesn't mean I can't have other relationships."

"Yes, but I would think you'd want to pick and choose those relationships very carefully."

"I do that anyway. You heard what Angie said. I haven't had a date in two years. That's not for lack of invitations."

Craig didn't doubt it. "So you're a discriminating lady. Why would you settle for dating a guy you can't possibly get serious about?"

"You mean, a guy who couldn't possibly get serious about me." She tugged her hand from his grasp and turned away from him. "It's Sandy, isn't it? Angie warned me that single men don't like to date women with babies."

He felt saddened by her attitude. "No, honey, it's not Sandy. It's you. You've got 'Mom' written all over you. It's in every word you speak and every move you make. You need a man who can be a husband and father—a family man. I can't be that man."

"You think I'm shopping for a father?" she asked, suddenly watchful and wary.

"No...but maybe you should be."

Judging from the troubled look on her face, he'd hit home. He wished like hell he didn't have to take this stand, but the one thing he couldn't do was mislead Isabel into believing he would ever take responsibility for a child—any child.

He struggled to think of something to say that would make things all right between them. Maybe if he explained his reasons...but she might try to change his thinking. And in his present state of mind, not to mention body, he was afraid she could do it.

They were both silent for a long time. When Isabel finally looked at him, there was a calm acceptance in her eyes. She laid her hand on his forearm. The touch sent shock waves through him, reminding him how badly he wanted to touch more than hands.

"Craig," she said softly. "You're right. It might not be politically correct for me to admit this, but I've been shopping for a husband and someone to be a father to my children since I was Angie's age."

"And you'll find him," Craig said, although the thought of Isabel happily married to some other man made him slightly sick to his stomach. "And when you do, you'll know he's the right one. And so will he."

Judging from her frown, his words hadn't given her any reassurance. "My break's almost over," she said, disentangling her hand from his and deliberately avoiding his gaze. She stood and brushed off the seat of her jeans. "I need to check on Sandy before I go back to work. Would you like to see her?"

"Oh, um..." He wanted to. In fact, it really surprised him how much he wanted to see that kid again. But alarms went off in his head.

Isabel's face fell. "Never mind. I understand."

"No, you don't," he said quickly. "I like children, I really do."

"You don't have to say that, you know," she said briskly, her chin jutting forward in that faintly challenging way of hers. "I'm not offended by people who aren't as crazy about babies as I am."

"I like children, babies included," he said again, more forcefully this time. "I'd like to see Sandy." Once more wouldn't hurt.

"But if you like children, then why..." She slapped her hand over her mouth. "Never mind. You've been more than up-front with me, and you don't deserve a grilling."

Back inside the diner, Isabel made hasty introductions to her parents, Hector and Patsy, and her two brothers Paulo and David. Apparently they were all familiar with Craig's role in Sandy's rescue, because they practically stood in line to pump his hand and slap him on the back.

"It was a fine thing you did, stopping to help my Izzy and the little infante," Hector said in slow, precise English, speaking for all of them. "We're glad you finally gave us the chance to thank you. Your dinner's on the house, okay?"

"Thanks, but that's not really necessary. Isabel already gave me a free breakfast." Craig realized too late just how scandalous that sounded. Three overprotective DeLeon men went from smiling to scowling in a fraction of a second.

Thankfully Isabel was there to save him, or he might have ended up with the imprint of his face on the grill. "After we finished with Sandy at the hospital, he drove me home and I asked him in and made him some eggs

Benedict," she said. "Give us a break, would ya? Come on, Craig, Sandy's back here."

Isabel led the way through a storeroom, down a dark hallway and into the small apartment that was attached to the restaurant. In the living room an elderly, elfin woman, with salt-and-pepper hair pulled back into a tight bun, sat in front of the television watching a Spanish-language station. A little girl, about two or three, sat dozing in her lap. An older boy, maybe four or five, sat cross-legged on the floor playing with a radio-controlled car.

Craig scanned the room for signs of Sandy, more anxious than he ought to be. He saw a blanket and a rattle on the sofa beside the woman, but no baby.

"Nanno," Isabel said in a loud voice as she turned down the TV, giving Craig a pretty good clue that the older woman was hard-of-hearing. The rest of the introduction was conducted in Spanish.

"Ah, Craig Jaeger," the older woman said as she shook the hand he offered with almost as much strength as her son and grandsons had shown. Nodding vigorously, she rattled something off in rapid Spanish.

Craig stared blankly at her. He knew only a few words of the language, enough to get by with some of his nonEnglish-speaking construction workers. "This goes here," "Put on your hard hat," "Friday is pay day." Not a very flexible vocabulary.

"No, Nanno, *no habla español,*" Isabel was saying. Then she shrugged apologetically at Craig. "She doesn't speak English, not a word, despite the fact that she's lived in this country for thirty-five years. But at least we all grew up bilingual. These are Paulo's two kids, Jesse and Alison."

Craig winked at the drowsy little girl and shook hands with the boy. "Have I met the whole DeLeon clan, now?" he asked Isabel, feeling a bit overwhelmed by the sheer number in her family.

"Oh, heavens, no. David has three children, home with their mother, I presume. And I have two more younger brothers. Angie's twin, Alonzo, is away at school. He goes to Trinity University in San Antonio. And Patrick...Patrick doesn't live close by anymore."

It was hard to miss the shadow that crossed Isabel's face when she mentioned the brother named Patrick, but she quickly recovered, not allowing time for questions.

"Nanno takes care of any little DeLeons whose parents work at the diner. She even takes in the other employees' kids, sometimes, if they find themselves without a sitter. I don't know what we'd do without her."

Craig had very dim memories of his own paternal grandmother, a stern old termagant who was always lecturing about not running in the house or putting sticky fingers on the furniture.

"This way," Isabel said, leading the way toward a door that led from the living room to a bedroom. She put a finger to her lips as she opened the door and stepped quietly inside the dimly lit nursery.

Sandy was there, in a crib in the corner of the room. She was lying on her stomach with her rump stuck up in the air, her thumb anchored in her mouth.

Craig's heart lodged in his throat at the sight of her, so content in her warm little crib and her pink cotton jammies, so *loved*. She was a far cry from that pitiful, naked waif abandoned on the beach. For the first time, the magnitude of what he and Isabel had done that March morning really hit him. They had saved a life.

What a lucky little girl Sandy was, at least for the moment. She had this big, warm, welcoming family to nestle in. He could only hope, for her sake, that whoever adopted her would give her even half of this love and security.

"Look at that head of hair," Craig whispered. "What are you doing, putting Rogain in her bottle?"

"That's just how little Mexican babies look," Isabel replied, ruffling the black wisps of hair which had already gone far past peach fuzz. "You should see *my* baby pictures. I looked like Moe from the *Three Stooges.*"

"She's getting prettier every day," Craig said. Realizing how sappy he was starting to sound, he shoved his thumbs in the pockets of his jeans and nodded toward the door. "I know you need to get back to work. Thanks for letting me take a peek at her."

"Any time. I love showing her off. Sometimes you'd think I actually gave birth to her, the way I carry on."

"You did something just as important. You gave her back her life, and I helped. Maybe it's pretentious of me to think so, but I feel like we did something pretty special."

Isabel stared at him incredulously, her eyes swimming with tears. "Oh, Craig, I didn't think...I wasn't sure...I mean, I'm so glad you feel that way. Sometimes I'm almost crushed by the enormity of what we did, and I didn't think anyone else understood it."

They stared at each other, snagged in a spiderweb of tension and indecision. Then she moved into his arms as naturally as if they'd been lovers for years, her face turned upward, her eyes dewy and trusting.

He didn't question what was happening, although perhaps he should have. His brain short-circuited and his instincts took over. He sought her mouth with his, found it and took possession, gently at first—holding back—then with less caution. She tasted faintly of coffee. He buried his hands in her thick hair and deepened the kiss, delving her depths with his tongue, excited by the way she opened to him so freely.

But even as he reeled from the heady mix of pleasure in the kiss and desire for more, he recognized that his attraction to Isabel was much more than physical. No matter how much he wanted to deny it, they had forged a bond that had a lot to do with the little bundle of sugar and spice asleep in the crib.

The idea scared the hell out of him. He hadn't felt this way since . . . well, since he'd first set eyes on his squalling infant brother and realized what an awesome responsibility had been placed on his shoulders.

This was different, he reminded himself. Sandy wasn't his responsibility. She didn't need him the way Tom had. She had Isabel. What child could ask for more?

Isabel sensed Craig's subtle pulling away about the same time her own feet touched ground. What in heaven's name was she doing? They'd just agreed they wouldn't be seeing each other again, and she'd promptly fallen into his arms, conveniently forgetting all the reasons they were so wrong for each other.

Still, there was something about the way he looked at Sandy, a softness that crept into his eyes when he talked about her, that touched her on a deep level. Why did he keep denying he wanted a family when it seemed so obvious that just the opposite was true? Maybe if she just gave him a little more space . . . maybe if he spent more time around Sandy, he could deal with whatever mental blocks he had about marrying and raising kids.

Or maybe she was just fooling herself. They'd agreed not to see each other. She should abide by that mutual decision.

She broke the kiss and gently extracted herself from Craig's embrace, folding her arms protectively around herself. "I really need to get back to work."

"I know. I'm sorry for keeping you."

They said no more as she walked him back to his place at the counter, totaled his bill and pointedly stuck it in her pocket. "When Papa offers to give you dinner on the house, you better take it," she said. "He might not ever be that generous again."

Craig smiled, and the flash of gleaming white teeth made Isabel's heart pound. He was so damn charming when he wanted to be. "Tell him thank-you," he said as he laid some money on the counter. "And don't argue about the tip."

He sauntered out of the diner without a backward glance. Isabel swallowed the painful lump in her throat. Was this it, then? She should let it go. But how could she, when she felt so inexplicably connected to him?

The moment he was out of sight, Isabel's mother abandoned her cash register and bustled over to Isabel. "Oh, honey, he is adorable," she said, gushing.

"That's not exactly the word I would use."

"All right, then, he's a hunk. Your sister said he was good-looking, but I never imagined! Did he ask you out again?"

"No." She tried to sound bored.

"Well, maybe he will," Patsy said, narrowing her eyes speculatively. "Wouldn't he make a nice son-in-

law, and a wonderful father for Sandy? Why, he's
just—"

"Whoa, whoa, whoa!" Isabel interrupted as she
pulled on her apron over her head. "You can forget all
that. Craig has made it very clear that he's not interested in marriage or family."

"Well," Patsy said, patting her red fluff of hair, "he
might change his mind. Men have been known to do
that. In fact, your father wasn't so keen on marriage.
He thought I was crazy—a *gringa* chasing after a
Latino. It wasn't so common back then, and he knew
we were in for trouble. But love won out. Maybe it will
for you, too, honey. You're not giving up, are you?"

Were her yearnings that plain? Isabel looked at her
mother. "No. No, I'm not giving up." She felt only a
small twinge of guilt over the plan that was taking
shape. She abhorred the thought of playing any kind of
cat-and-mouse game with Craig, especially when he'd
been so honest with her. But she'd never before felt so
strong an urge to be with a man.

She wouldn't push, she promised herself. But she intended to give him every opportunity to change his
mind.

# Five

In the construction trailer at Blue Waters, Isabel sat on a battered vinyl couch that was so badly sprung it threatened to swallow her. Every time she leaned back, she tipped so far that her feet came off the floor. How was she supposed to maintain her professional dignity under such circumstances?

She'd done presentations before, lots of them, and she usually breezed through them with poise and confidence. But even without the woman-eating couch, she would have had trouble staying cool in the presence of these three men. They bombarded her with questions and scrutinized her drawings down to the last detail, like they were searching for some weakness, waiting for her to falter.

The most imposing of the tribunal was Sinclair Jaeger, Craig's father and spokesman for the Blue Waters developers. He was a tall, angular man who, although still handsome in his late sixties, bore little resemblance to his son. He had the sharp, darting eyes of a lion on the hunt, and deep grooves around his mouth that indicated a perpetual frown. His questions to Isabel were brusque and to the point, just short of rude.

The second man was the construction foreman, Bill Powers, whose role seemed to be that of devil's advocate, although he clearly wasn't a major decision-maker in the group. Isabel got the idea that he'd been asked to sit in on this meeting to buffer the obvious tension between father and son.

The third man was, of course, Craig Jaeger. The suspicious way he stared at her was almost worse than the challenging questions his father kept shooting at her.

Isabel had acted on Craig's suggestion to bid on decorating his model condos. He probably hadn't expected her to follow up, given the way things had been left between them. But she had, hoping their business contact would reopen some doors that should never have been slammed shut. She'd shamelessly cut her profit margin to the nubs on the bid, too, in order to give Craig every reason to hire her.

Her strategy had worked. If she survived this grilling, the job was hers. But the black look on Craig's face was giving her second thoughts.

"Well, Ms. DeLeon," Sinclair finally said, "I have just one more question for you. Can you have everything ready by July Fourth?"

July Fourth was only a month away. Isabel had just toured the three units she would be decorating. They were barely roughed in. "When do you expect the units to be ready for the furnishings?" She directed the question to Craig.

"About three weeks," he said, like he expected her to object, and indeed, she wanted to. That would give her less than a week to have everything in place. But she'd worked on tighter schedules.

"If I can have six full days, I should have no problems," she said with more confidence than she felt.

Sinclair nodded, then looked at the other two men. "Any problem meeting that timetable?"

"We can do it," Bill said. Craig didn't object, but neither did he agree.

"Fine, then." Sinclair stood and offered his hand to Isabel. "Ms. DeLeon, you have the job. Now, who's for lunch? I hear that seafood restaurant on the old ship is good."

"I'm sorry, I can't," Isabel said automatically. "But thank you." Sinclair unnerved her, and she didn't intend to spend any more time with him than she had to.

"You two go ahead," Craig said to the other men. "I have just a couple of details I'd like to thrash out with Ms. DeLeon."

The gazes of father and son clashed for a split second before Sinclair nodded, although he looked anything but pleased.

As soon as Craig and Isabel were alone, he jumped up from his chair and began pacing the small office like a criminal prosecutor interrogating a witness. "So, why'd you do it?"

Isabel refused to let him intimidate her. "Why'd I bid for the job? You're the one who suggested it."

"That was before we decided not to see each other. This is going to be awkward at best."

"You didn't have to hire me," she countered.

"It wasn't entirely my decision to make."

Isabel was quickly tiring of the verbal sparring. "Look, Craig, this is a job I wanted, and I'll do it well. We won't have to see much of each other if you're uncomfortable—" She cut herself off. "No, wait a minute. I might as well be honest. I went after this job so I'd have an excuse to see you again. I couldn't seem to... stop myself."

Craig halted his pacing and stared down at her. "We agreed it would be best if we didn't see each other," he said, the words seeming forced.

"I know what we agreed. But something inside me won't let it go. I feel like we're making a terrible mistake." Somehow she found the bravado to speak her mind completely. "I've never been so attracted to a man in my life. Never."

The fight seemed to go out of him. With a weary sigh he sat down on the couch next to her—but not too close, she noticed. "I feel the same way about you. But, Isabel—"

"I know what you're going to say. I'm looking for one thing, and you're something else altogether. But maybe you're not what you think you are."

"Isabel—"

"I mean, people change. Have you ever been in love?"

His eyes took on a blatant wariness. "No, I don't believe I have."

"Neither have I. But I know from talking to my parents, and watching my brothers and their wives, that love changes people. Even Angie. You should have seen her before she had Corey—irresponsible, undependable and convinced that motherhood was the worst possible curse. Corey has turned her into a regular little Super Mom.

"Now, as far as you and I go..." She hesitated, knowing she was on shaky ground. But Craig was listening intently, so she plunged ahead. "You can't deny there's chemistry between us, and at least the *potential* for love. And if it should happen...well, miracles can follow, that's what I think." She took a deep breath. She was making a complete fool of herself.

"You won't change my mind about marriage and family," he said point-blank. Although he had every right to be irritated by her assumptions, his tone was apologetic.

"You're right, *I* won't change your mind. And I wouldn't try, honestly. But you never know, your mind might change on its own. I just have this feeling about you...." She paused. How could she explain what she'd seen in his eyes as he'd gazed at Sandy sleeping in her crib?

"You've met my father," Craig said. "You've seen what a glowing example he set for me as a parent. My brother and I were raised by a houseful of servants, a constantly changing sea of faces. And, Isabel, I'm so much like Sinclair it scares me."

*You're nothing like him,* she wanted to say. Perhaps outwardly they were similar. They were both ambitious, successful businessmen, owners of their own companies, putting in too many hours at work. But there was at least one fundamental difference between the two men. Isabel saw compassion in Craig's eyes, whereas she'd seen nothing but hard cynicism in Sinclair's.

But Craig wasn't going to listen to her. Some things he would simply have to see for himself and learn on his own. Instead, she focused on something else he'd said. "Your brother? I didn't know you had a brother."

"I don't, not anymore," Craig said in a monotone. "Tom died about four years ago."

"I'm sorry." Her heart went out to him. Although she knew it was folly to touch him, she did it anyway. She'd been raised in a family of touchers and huggers, and it was impossible for her to sit next to him, witness his pain and do nothing to comfort him. She laid one hand gently over his. "You must have been very close."

He shook his head. "Not close enough."

His words puzzled her, but, sensing the depth of pain behind his stoic mask, she chose not to probe too deeply, not today. She was already treading in water way above her head. Seeking firm footing, she retreated to the less personal venue of business. "What's so special about July Fourth?" she asked, tactfully withdrawing her hand.

He seemed relieved by the change of subject. "The developers want to do the grand opening that weekend," he said with a careless shrug. "They're planning a big beach party with free soft drinks and hot dogs, volleyball..." He was looking at her mouth.

"Sounds great."

"There'll be a radio station remote broadcast, beer sponsorship, the whole nine... You see, that's why this is so awkward. I can't even hold onto my train of thought, because all I can think about is kissing you."

"What?" Her skin suddenly tingled with awareness, and she could swear every breath of air had been sucked out of her lungs. "What did you say?" The words came out in a whisper.

"You heard me right. The whole time you were giving that presentation, so cool, so elegant, I was wondering what it would be like to pull the pins out of your hair and watch it fall over your shoulders."

His hands followed his words, pulling out her carefully anchored hairpins one by one. She was helpless to stop him. She wasn't even sure she wanted him to stop. She had deliberately pushed her way back into his life, knowing how strong the attraction was between them. She had known this would happen.

He leaned closer, so that his breath tickled her hair. As always, his nearness ignited fiery trails of longing inside her body. She moistened her lips with her tongue, nervous but hungry for his kiss, aching for the touch she knew he longed to give.

He slipped one hand beneath her hair to the back of her neck and pulled her the rest of the way, closing the distance between them. His possession of her mouth was swift and sure, packed with more feeling than any one kiss had a right to. The sudden influx of emotions made her dizzy, and she found herself clinging to his shoulders for support, positive that if she released him she would slide right onto the floor. The warmth of his body enveloped her as his lips and tongue worked their magic, transporting her to another dimension.

Showing more control than she, he ended the kiss, brushed her cheek with his and nuzzled her ear. "I'm a bad risk, Isabel. I'm a workaholic from a fractured family. I have nothing to offer you. Nothing but this." He kissed her again.

"It's enough," she murmured against his lips when they paused for a few labored gasps, amazed she could formulate words at all. "It's enough for now."

"For now and forever." His intense, blue-gray gaze seared her all the way to her soul. "Don't pin any expectations on me. Please. You have to understand that, or this won't work."

"I won't expect anything more than you're capable of giving. But I can hope. You can't stop me from hoping."

He kissed her lightly on the neck, just below her ear, and his hand skimmed over her breast. "I want to make love to you," he said, his voice rough.

"Now?" she squeaked.

"Not now. Soon, though. I won't ask for more than you're willing to give, either. But you can be damn sure I'll be hoping, too."

Isabel got more than she bargained for with the Blue Waters models. The construction crew gave her only four days instead of the six she'd demanded, and Craig had offered her a substantial bonus if she could still make the July Fourth deadline. Of course, she'd accepted the challenge.

Craig, perhaps uncertain of her ability to finish the job on time, never left her side. So she took advantage of his capable help, asking him to do everything from laying carpet to fetching lunch.

Unfortunately, his presence was often more of a hindrance than a help, although through no fault of his own. Isabel had a hell of a time keeping her mind on business when he was constantly within reaching distance, looking all male in his soft, faded jeans and work shirts. Thanks to the distraction, she'd already mismeasured wallpaper, put the wrong drapes up in one bedroom and dropped a dish on the quarry-tiled kitchen floor, shattering it into a thousand pieces.

Every once in a while, during an unguarded moment, she caught him giving her a distinctly predatory look that unnerved her completely.

Over the past month they'd spent a lot of time together and not all of it business-related. True to his
word, Craig hadn't asked her for more than she was
ready to give when it came to physical intimacy. But she
felt her reserve crumbling away by the minute.

At 10:30 p.m. on July third, she and Craig were the
only ones left at Blue Waters, putting the finishing
touches on the decor of the last model. Isabel had
transformed the two-bedroom condo into a lavish English country cottage, complete with mahogany antiques and floral chintz upholstery, hunt prints on the
walls, Turkish carpets on the floor—all bearing the
warm patina of many years of gentle use. No detail had
been overlooked, from the Blue Willow china and vintage table linens in the dining room to scented soaps in
the bath to a family-portrait gallery—old photos and
tintypes picked up at flea markets—in the hallway.

Now all that remained was to dress the bed in the
master bedroom, a chore Isabel had put off until last,
hoping she could send Craig home and do it by herself.
But no such luck. He apparently felt obligated to stay
until the last detail was in place.

With a resigned sigh, Isabel tossed a feather pillow at
Craig, which he snagged in a deft one-handed catch. He
gave her a questioning look. "Are you trying to start a
pillow fight?"

"No. Put the pillow slips on while I do the sheets,"
she directed briskly. "Please," she added. During the
course of the stressful day she had let common cour-
tesy fly out the window, behaving like a dictator in her
effort to meet the deadline. Craig had withstood it all
without a single complaint.

With a mischievous smile he tossed the pillow back at her. "A pillow fight sounds like more fun. So many feather pillows for one bed. What a temptation."

"Don't even think about it." She cringed at the thought of vacuuming up goose down from all over the condo.

Craig walked around the bed and moved behind her, placing his hands on her shoulders and beginning a slow, sensual massage. "Lighten up, Isabel," he said softly against her hair. "I was only kidding."

She sighed, taking pleasure in the feel of his strong fingers kneading the stiff muscles in her neck and shoulders.

"We're almost done," he continued, his voice low and seductive. "The models look fantastic, and tomorrow you get to relax, spend time with Sandy. You should be feeling pretty proud of yourself right about now."

She was. And she would celebrate—as soon as the ordeal of the bed was behind them. She gradually relaxed, loosening the death grip she had on the pillow.

"Better?" Craig asked, giving her shoulders one final squeeze.

"Mmm." It was all she could manage.

He took the pillow from her and reached for a stack of pressed pillowcases.

Isabel started with the fitted sheet, which was patterned in romantic pink cabbage roses, smoothing the soft cotton across the mattress and thinking that what she'd really like to do was crawl onto the bed and pull Craig with her. She did the flat sheet next, struggling to keep her attention on her task instead of watching Craig as he wrestled with pillowcases and shams, his masculinity showcased magnificently against the feminine frills.

At last she threw the satin comforter over the bed and began arranging the pillows at the head. Craig handed her the last one, then watched with a critical eye as she climbed up on the high mattress and placed the pillow just so.

"A little to the right," he said.

"You think?" She complied, studying the results.

"And now that one with the gold tassles on it. It should go below the pink ruffled one."

She started to follow his directions when she heard the low rumble of his laughter, which he tried unsuccessfully to disguise with a cough. She whacked him over the head with the pillow in question. "That's not funny."

"Yes it is. You arrange pillows like an artist arranging a still life. Does it really make that much difference?"

She puffed out her chest in mock umbrage. "How dare you question my decorating abilities. Of course it makes a difference. The subtlest detail can influence a potential buyer's impression of the entire condo."

"Oh, well in that case, let's do something entirely different with the pillows."

"What?" she asked, suspicious of his suddenly serious tone.

Before the word was even out of her mouth, he'd pounced. She found herself flat on her back amidst the mountain of pillows with Craig on top of her kissing the daylights out of her. Her ability to resist was nonexistent. Hadn't she been fantasizing this scene only minutes ago? She melted into a kiss, losing herself in the feel of his mouth, the firm strokes of his tongue and his hands lightly skimming her body, leaving trails of fire in their wake.

A pulsing need deep at her center, which had made itself known quite often lately, expanded in waves to encompass her whole body. Isabel knew, in some far recess of her mind, that she should stop, that despite the closeness she felt with Craig, despite all the time they'd spent together, she wasn't emotionally prepared to yield her body completely to him. But that small objection was no match for her raging hormones. Clothes would have started to fly if the doorbell hadn't rung.

"Who's that?" she asked, frustration warring with relief.

Craig didn't seem at all surprised that someone was at the door at this hour of the evening. He pulled back, his face full of regret, and gave her one final, gentle kiss. "It's a surprise. Finish up this bed, and then meet me in the dining room."

It took a few moments for Isabel to pull herself together, make her arms and legs work properly. But she finally managed to straighten the bed linen and pile up the pillows. As she worked, she heard muffled voices and the front door closing, then smelled a delectable aroma. After giving the comforter one final pat and a last, longing glance over her shoulder, she hurried to the dining room.

There she found the most beautifully laid out meal she'd ever seen—chicken Kiev, salad, hot rolls, chilled wine, candlelight and flowers.

"Since we worked through dinner, I thought you might be hungry. So I called an after-hours caterer," Craig explained as he held out her chair.

She had a million objections on the tip of her tongue. They weren't supposed to be eating from the antique china, which was rented. If they broke anything, they'd have to pay for it. Same went for stains on the linen.

And when they were done with their meal, they would have to wash everything and put it back in order. But all of that seemed insignificant in the face of Craig's thoughtful, *romantic* gesture.

She sat down with murmured thanks.

The meal was exquisite, and Isabel devoured the whole experience—the excellent food, the wine, the soft candlelight and her incredibly gorgeous dining companion. She found herself fantasizing that this was *their* home, and that Sandy was sleeping in the next room. And when they were done with dinner, they would return to that four-poster bed and all the satin and ruffles....

But Craig surprised her. Although he could have easily pressed his considerable advantage, when they finished the meal he sent her home with a kiss and a promise that he would return the condo to its previously pristine condition before heading for bed himself. As she drove home, her body still thrumming with desire, she wondered if perhaps Craig didn't have a lot more sense than she did.

The Fourth of July dawned bright and clear with the promise of temperatures in the high eighties—perfect for the Blue Waters grand opening. Craig made the rounds one last time from the beach concession stands to the marina, built around a newly dredged lagoon, to the model condos and back to the VIP tent, assuring himself that everything was in order.

It wasn't even noon, yet, and crowds were already starting to gather on the beach, lured by the prospect of free food and drink, no doubt. But the person Craig most wanted to see hadn't yet arrived.

Isabel's family, she'd told him, always celebrated the Fourth by closing the restaurant and barbecuing in the backyard. It was an event she wouldn't miss, but she'd promised she'd stop by Blue Waters for a while.

Relief and anticipation washed over him when he saw her red Grand Am rolling into the parking lot. During the past few weeks he'd seen her almost every day despite their frantic schedules. Sometimes it was only for a hasty lunch of fast-food in the trailer, with construction workers barging in and out. Sometimes they managed dinner together, usually with Sandy in tow. And once, just once, they'd slipped away for a moonlight swim in the ocean.

Afterward, laughing and breathless, they had lain on the sand and necked like a couple of teenagers. He had slipped the strap of her swimsuit over her shoulder and brought one breast out into the moonlight, delighting in her sensitivity to his hands, and then his mouth. She had quivered and moaned beneath him. He could still taste the salty ocean on her skin.

Last night they'd come even closer to crossing the line.

Each time he saw her, he wanted her more—all of her, not just her sexy body. He couldn't get enough of her sunny smiles, her intelligence, her closeness to that big, wonderful family. And her foster child. Damn, but her single-minded devotion to Sandy was probably the thing he adored most about her.

He looked forward to actually having her to himself for several hours today—and no wallpaper or pictures to hang. He had made it clear to anyone who cared that, come noon he was off the clock, and he was damn sure going to spend some of his leisure time with Isabel. A little sand, a little surf and definitely some fireworks....

His musings were interrupted when he realized there were three other cars following closely on Isabel's bumper. Craig could hardly believe it when he saw the whole DeLeon clan piling out of those cars, complete with coolers, beach umbrellas, baby strollers and lawn chairs.

With Sandy draped over one shoulder and a huge diaper bag over the other, Isabel led the parade toward the beach.

Craig met them halfway. "Hello, there—here, let me carry something." He reached for the diaper bag, but Isabel handed him Sandy instead. The baby was wearing a red-white-and-blue sundress, a floppy, big-brimmed hat and tiny blue high-top sneakers. And she felt heavy. "Good heavens, this little girl is gaining weight like a sumo wrestler."

Sandy didn't seem to mind the insult, awarding him with a big, toothless smile.

"Hi, yourself," Isabel said with a laugh. "In case you're wondering why I brought an entourage, Papa decided he didn't want to cook as long as there was free food available, so we opted to join our party to yours. Hope you don't mind."

"The more the merrier."

She awarded him a grateful smile.

Damn, she was gorgeous. He looked her over, subtly. He didn't want Hector to catch him ogling his daughter. Still, it was hard not to ogle. She was wearing a short terry-cloth romper that showed off her shapely legs.

Although he could easily have devoted all of his attention to Isabel, Craig remembered his manners long enough to make a little small talk with Isabel's parents, shake hands with her brothers and meet their wives and a couple more grandkids. Even Alonzo, Angie's twin, had taken a break from summer school to partake in the family celebration. The only one missing was the mysterious brother Patrick, and no one mentioned him.

Every time Craig turned around, someone was handing him a baby to hold. He would have thought it a well-organized plot to convince him of his fitness as a family man, but for the worried expression that had taken over Isabel's face.

"Let's go check on the models," Isabel suggested to Craig once everyone was settled. "I want to make sure none of the wallpaper is peeling up and that all the plants are still alive." She put Sandy in Patsy's lap, much to Craig's relief. He had grown fond of the little munchkin despite his best efforts, but this might be his only chance to spend a few minutes alone with Isabel.

As soon as they were out of earshot of the family, Isabel gave a helpless shrug. "I'm sorry about that. We pass kids around like sacks of potatoes in my family. It hardly ever occurs to us that not everyone is as enthralled with DeLeon children as we are."

"I didn't mind."

She smiled then. "They like you, you know."

"Your family likes me? They hardly know me."

"No, I mean, kids like you. They always go right to you, and they never cry when you hold them."

"So I should have a dozen of my own, is that it?"

She stopped in her tracks. "Oh, Craig, I didn't mean that. Don't be reading ulterior motives into my every word. I was just making an observation, that's all. And it wasn't my idea to bring the whole family here. I would have preferred a little quiet time with you, alone."

He felt like an ogre. "I didn't mean to jump down your throat. I guess I'm a little sensitive. And we can still have some quiet time. Do we really need to check the models?"

"No, I guess not. I assume we'll hear about it if anything's gone wrong."

"Good. I want to show you something."

They headed up the stairs that led from the beach to the attractive stucco building, which was on stilts. Craig pulled a key from the pocket of his white tennis shorts as he led Isabel up another flight of stairs, to the only unit in the four-plex she hadn't decorated.

"Oh! I thought this one wasn't finished," Isabel said as Craig ushered her inside the living room, with its white walls, beige carpet and modest rental furniture.

"It's mine," he announced. "I know the decor isn't quite up to your standards, but it beats a bed pushed to the back of the construction trailer."

"And why, pray tell, did you lure me into your lair, Mr. Jaeger?" She laughed gently, and the sound caressed his senses. She had only to tilt her head a certain way or look at him with those sexy, almond-shaped eyes of hers and he went hard all the way to his toes.

He smiled wickedly. "Quiet time."

Although she continued to smile, she didn't appear altogether comfortable. Hell, what did she think, that he actually brought her here to seduce her? All right, so the thought had crossed his mind. But mostly he just wanted to be with her.

"So this is your home away from home," she said, walking around the living room, examining it with a critical eye. "I could help you pick out some pictures for the walls."

"I won't be here long enough to warrant an investment in art," he said, belatedly realizing how cavalier he sounded—like he couldn't wait to get away from Galveston.

"Oh? How long do you expect the construction to take?" she asked. She tried to make it sound like a casual question, but he could hear the strain in her voice.

"Phase Two should be finished by Thanksgiving."

"And then you'll go back to Dallas?"

"That's the plan." Unless he could pick up another job down here. He'd submitted some designs for a proposed medical office complex on the north side of town, thinking he might extend his visit a few more months. He didn't want to examine his motives too carefully. Nor did he want to tell Isabel about it until his plans were firmer. Their relationship could only withstand so much uncertainty. "You want some lemonade?" he asked.

"Yes. No. Oh, Craig, I don't know." She sank down into one of the armchairs.

"Isabel, what's wrong?" He was appalled to find her close to tears. Hell, she'd known all along that he made his permanent home in Dallas. And Thanksgiving was a long way away. Even he could admit that a lot could happen in five months. "Would you prefer root beer?"

"This is serious, Craig. You talk so blithely about moving away, and it made me realize that we really do have different agendas."

He'd known that all along.

"I've been putting off telling you about something, sort of waiting for the right moment, but I'm beginning to think you'll be packed up and gone before that moment ever arrives."

He didn't like the sound of this. "What is it, honey?"

"I really can't postpone it any longer. Who knows when the state will start its investigation?"

"What investigation?"

"The one that will decide whether I'm a good prospective mother. I've applied to adopt Sandy."

Craig's mouth dropped open, first in surprise, then in delight. He knelt beside her chair and took her hand. "Oh, Isabel, I think that's great."

"You do?"

"You'll be a wonderful mother for Sandy. Frankly, I've been a little worried about who would be chosen to adopt her—and how you would handle it when you had to give her up. But if you're willing to take her on permanently, there's nothing to worry about. No one could find anything lacking in your home, or the environment you provide for Sandy."

"Tell that to the state."

"Is there a problem?"

"Yes, a big one. There's a young Hispanic couple who's had an application in for a baby girl for a long time. Sandy would be ideal."

"But Sandy's been with you since the day she was born. She's obviously well taken care of. They wouldn't take her away from you, would they?"

"They might. You see, this couple has something really important for Sandy that I'm lacking."

"What? What could that child possibly be lacking?"

When she answered, her words were barely audible. "A f-father."

"Oh." He felt like he'd been kicked in the solar plexus, because he knew what was coming next, and there was no way to escape it anymore than he could escape the sun setting in the west at the end of the day. "Does this mean you're giving me the boot?" His voice was harsher than he intended, and with his next words

he struggled to sound more casual. "I understand. You
can hardly be expected to find a husband with your
boyfriend hanging around."

"No, Craig, you don't understand. You're the most
perfectly qualified man I can think of. I want you to
marry me."

# Six

Isabel could hardly believe she'd just blurted out a marriage proposal. Was she out of her mind? She should have waited. She should have eased Craig into the idea. But the way he'd talked so casually about returning to Dallas had scared her.

And now she'd scared Craig, judging from the look of sheer panic on his face. He sank onto the sofa opposite her, his movements jerky, as if his legs refused to hold him up any longer, and his complexion had gone from a healthy tan to a peaked beige.

"*Marry* you?" he repeated.

"That's . . . what I said."

"After everything I've told you about me, and knowing how I feel about . . . ?"

"Yes."

He was shaking his head. "Then you must not have been paying attention. I'm not good husband material.

I'm a workaholic. Just look how hard we've had to struggle this past month to steal even a few minutes together—"

"And how wonderful those few minutes have been. You can't deny that."

He closed his eyes and squeezed his hands together until she could see the outline of every corded muscle in his forearms. "No, I can't deny that," he agreed. "But we're not married. Marriage is something that has to be worked at. It takes an investment of time and effort— neither of which I can promise."

"I can work hard enough for the both of us." She knew she sounded desperate, and so she was. She struggled to find the inner calm she would need to make him understand. "Craig, lots of husbands travel and put in long hours. Granted, it's not ideal, but it can work. We may not have a lot of time together, but the quality of that time is what's important."

"It's not just the time commitment." He stood and walked to the glass door that looked out onto the beach. He stared out at the ocean for a long time, running his hand through his thick, midnight hair over and over before finally completing his thought. "Some men just aren't meant to be husbands and fathers."

"Why do you believe that about yourself?" she asked, incredulous.

"I don't believe it, I *know* it."

"How, if you've never tried marriage? You...you haven't, have you?"

He turned back toward her, and his face was so full of misery it squeezed her heart. "No. But I won't 'try' with you and Sandy. I won't see either of you punished for the rest of your lives simply because you need a husband so bad you would marry any jerk who walked in off the street.''

She rose to her feet, her cheeks hot and her eyes burning with unshed tears. "Now you listen to me, Craig Jaeger. If I were willing to marry any jerk off the street, don't you think I could have found one before now? The streets are full of men."

"Then why didn't you latch onto one?"

"Because none of them was right."

"And neither am I." His expression softened, and he walked toward her. For a moment she thought he was going to touch her, but he stopped before he got close enough to do that. "Honey, it's only because I care about both of you that I'm saying no. You deserve better."

She folded her arms and looked down at her feet. "Maybe so. Maybe I deserve a man who loves me and is committed to being the best damn husband and father he can be—one who will come home at night and play with the baby while I fix dinner. A man who would always be there for me. One who would satisfy me in every way."

When she glanced up, she saw a look on Craig's face that defied interpretation. Yearning? Frustration? Whatever he was feeling, he quickly schooled his features to a neutral expression the moment their gazes met.

"That's exactly what you need," he said, the words barely above a choked whisper. "Not only a man who'll love you, but one *you* can love without reservation."

"Then I'll keep looking," she said, wondering if he thought it impossible that she could love *him*. She met his gaze with a defiant one of her own. "But they'll probably take Sandy away from me before I find him."

She left then, because if she hadn't she would have made an even greater fool of herself by bawling. As she ran down both flights of steps, tears blurring her vision, she half expected to hear the thud of his tennis shoes behind her. But he didn't follow.

Isabel made her way down the beach a good distance from the blaring radio music and all those happy, laughing people. She slipped off her sandals and walked down to the water, letting the waves lap over her bare feet and the wind dry her tears. After a few minutes of cleansing solitude, she was able to review the scene that had just taken place with some objectivity.

At least she'd been honest with Craig. She had that going for her. As for the rest of her performance, she wasn't very proud of it. She had tried to manipulate a man into marrying her by sending him on a guilt trip. Yes, she was desperate. She would do anything to keep Sandy. That didn't make what she'd done any more noble.

When Isabel felt more in control, she returned to where her family was gathered and made a beeline for Sandy. The baby sat in Patsy's lap, both of them shaded by an umbrella. As soon as Patsy saw Isabel, she immediately relinquished the child—almost as if she instinctively knew that her daughter needed to hold the baby and feel close to her.

Isabel settled onto a towel in the sand and rubbed her cheek against Sandy's soft, shiny black hair.

"Man trouble?" Patsy whispered. Not that the others could hear over the noisy game of volleyball they'd started.

"How could you tell?" Isabel replied grimly. "Oh, Mama, I just made a complete idiot of myself. I asked Craig to marry me."

Patsy greeted that news with a long silence. "I didn't know things were getting so serious between you two."

"They weren't. I mean, it could have gotten serious, if I'd given it more time. But I don't have time. Sandy needs a father."

"And is that how you asked him? 'Sandy needs a father, you're handy, let's get hitched?' No wonder he turned you down."

"It wasn't quite like that," Isabel objected.

"Do you love him?" Patsy asked. "Because it's no good marrying someone you don't love, even for the best of reasons."

"I do love him," Isabel answered. It was the first time she'd admitted it, even to herself, and the thought made her chest ache with regret. "But I doubt he wants to hear that. He seems frightened to death of the whole idea. It's so weird, Mama. It's like he really wants to be a family man but he's afraid to want it, so he pretends he doesn't. And I don't understand why."

"Could be any number of reasons," Patsy said, tapping her chin thoughtfully with one forefinger. "What's his family like?"

"He doesn't talk much about it. I know his mother died when he was ten, and his brother died just a few years ago. And he doesn't get along well with his father. You'd think a man who's been without real family for all those years would *want* one."

"Maybe, maybe not. Could be he's afraid of being happy. Some people are, you know."

Isabel could almost believe that. Craig was certainly afraid of something. "But why?"

"Happiness has its downside. When you're happy, sometimes you wonder whether you deserve to be, whether fate will take it all away from you in the blink of an eye."

Isabel couldn't imagine. "Have *you* ever felt like that?" Her parents' marriage had always seemed so perfect to her—full of love and laughter during the good times, and quiet strength during the bad.

"Sure. When I was pregnant with your brother Patrick. I remember thinking, 'I have a wonderful husband and three beautiful children—what if *this* one changes everything?"

"And darned if he didn't," Isabel murmured. "Have you heard from him lately?"

"As long as we send him money every couple of weeks, we don't hear a word. Thank God." She shivered delicately. "So what are you going to do, now that you've scared off the only marriage prospect you've had in years?"

"Mama! You shouldn't joke—"

"I'm only joking because I'm pretty sure he'll be back. I've seen the way he looks at you. A man doesn't look at a woman like that and then walk away, not unless he's suddenly turned into a piece of granite."

"How does he look at me?" Isabel asked with a skeptical tilt to her head.

"Like a man who feels something deep in his gut," Patsy said matter-of-factly. "Go on with you, now. Go have some fun and stop brooding. Why don't you join the volleyball game?"

She shook her head. Now that Sandy was in her arms, she didn't want to let her go.

"Then take Sandy down to the water and see what she thinks of it. You could use a little sun, too. You look pale."

Isabel's eyebrows flew up. "Who's calling who pale?"

Patsy laughed. "But I'm always pale. You used to get brown as a berry in the summer."

"Sun worshiping's not allowed anymore. But you're right, a few rays wouldn't hurt."

Isabel crossed the narrow strip of sun-warmed beach to the water's edge and dangled Sandy so that her toes just brushed the wet sand. Whenever a wave came toward them, she swung the baby up and out of the way just in time, making her coo excitedly—almost like she wanted to laugh. She was growing so fast, developing a distinct personality.

Isabel savored the moment, as she savored all their special moments together. By next summer, Sandy might be spending her days at the beach with someone else.

From a distant vantage point on the beach, Craig watched Isabel play with Sandy. They were building a sand castle. The baby was nestled in the triangle of Isabel's crossed legs. Every so often Isabel would dribble water from her fingers onto Sandy's bare foot, and the child would wave her hands excitedly.

The sight brought a lump to his throat. Had there ever been a woman and child who so surely belonged together? And yet, because of idiotic bureaucratic red tape, some self-important social worker could decide to rip the child from her home, just because there was no father present.

Oddly enough, he didn't think the lack of a father would hurt Sandy one bit. Better no father than one who isn't there, who doesn't care...or one whose presence is harmful. With Isabel as her mother, Sandy would have at least one loving, devoted parent. Without Isabel, who knew? Who could tell what kind of parents this supposedly ideal Hispanic couple might turn out to be?

He'd been thinking about her proposal. He hadn't reacted very well, but she'd really shocked the hell out of him. Now that he'd had time to consider her dilemma, he'd come up with a possible solution—if she was still speaking to him.

She didn't see him coming until his shadow blocked her sun. Then she looked up, her expression wary. "Hi."

"Hi. Need an architect for your castle?"

"I guess I do. It's pretty sorry looking."

"But not unsalvageable." He sat down next to her. "What you need are some thicker walls and a deeper moat. May I?"

"Be my guest."

They worked together in silence for a while, digging into wet sand with bare hands—fingers brushing innocently, then not so innocently—while patting it into place and sculpting miniature towers and bridges.

"Isabel."

"Please don't say anything. Maybe we can just forget I ever mentioned the *M* word."

"I can't forget it. In fact, I've thought about nothing else. We can't let them take Sandy away from you."

"Perhaps they won't." Her voice was so dull, Craig knew she didn't believe her own words. She began to busily untie and tie the strings on Sandy's bonnet. Sandy, dozing with her head pillowed against Isabel's thigh, was oblivious.

"What if..." he began carefully, his heart pounding like thunder inside his chest, "what if we were married strictly on paper?"

Her hands stilled. "You mean get married, but don't live together?"

He could already tell it was a bad idea, but he felt compelled to rationalize the suggestion. "Just until the adoption's final. Then we could get a quickie divorce. I have a lawyer friend who could—"

"No." The single word sliced through the air like a machete. "It's not that I don't appreciate the offer, but I don't take marriage vows that lightly. And divorce is out of the question."

Of course, it would be. He should have known that. Isabel had been raised a Roman Catholic, and she still went to church every Sunday with her family. "An annulment, then."

"On what grounds?"

"If the marriage were never consummated..." Good grief, what was he suggesting? To be married to Isabel and never make love to her? He *was* human, after all.

Craig felt tremendous relief when she shook her head. "Even if I could condone such an arrangement, it wouldn't work," she said. "The state does very thorough investigations. A paper marriage wouldn't fool them, and I couldn't lie about it, anyway. But thank you." She managed a wan smile, then leaned over and kissed his cheek, probably totally unaware of what the simple gesture did to him. Her warm lips against his jaw, the brief waft of her scent, even the sound of her breath, made the longing well up inside of him.

This was the damnedest situation he'd ever been in. He'd turned down her proposal and she'd turned down his, both in the course of an hour. It would be impossible for them to become intimate now. And yet he'd never wanted any woman like he did Isabel. He wanted to possess her, body and soul. He wanted to be the one she turned to in the night. He wanted to protect her and cherish her and make wild love to her.

And he wanted to help her keep that kid.

Given all that, did he have much choice?

"Isabel . . ."

"We don't have to talk about it anymore. I understand your position, sort of, and I think you understand mine. You can leave if you want."

"I don't want. Oh, hell, honey, let's do it."

"Do what?" she said, her eyes large with alarm.

"Let's get married. If it'll help you to keep Sandy, let's just do it."

"You mean, really? A real marriage?"

"As real as it needs to be to satisfy the state. But, Isabel, I can't promise you forever."

"Oh." That disturbing dullness crept into her voice again. "You still want to get divorced after the adoption is final."

"An annulment. Surely there are grounds besides not consummating."

"Yes, there are," she agreed cautiously. "In fact, the church has made it pretty darned easy to end a marriage and still be a 'good Catholic.'"

"I know it's not ideal," he said. "But at least it's a way for you to keep Sandy. Afterward, you'll still be free to find Mr. Right." The magnitude of what he was doing hit him in the chest like a blow with a sledgehammer. "I don't propose marriage very often, Isabel. I think you'd better accept."

She stared up at him with those brown eyes and dared him to take it back. But the longer she stared, the more certain he became that he was doing the right thing.

"Okay," she said.

He felt strangely nervous, now that the hard part was over. "Should I get on one knee, or what?"

"It's a little late for that."

"Then, may I kiss the bride-to-be?"

Her nod was almost imperceptible.

He touched her chin with sandy fingertips, gently tilting her face upward, and lowered his mouth to hers. As always, the first taste of her sent a white-hot bolt of electricity zinging through his body. Soon she would be his wife. He could lie with her every night, kiss her every morning when he woke up. The thought was much more appealing than it should have been.

Isabel responded to his kiss in a deliciously familiar way, meeting the bold thrust of his tongue with her own, sliding one sand-gritty hand along his chest and around to the back of his neck as she held onto the baby with the other. They were in full view of anyone on the beach who cared to notice, including the DeLeon clan, but Craig didn't care. They were engaged. Who could object to a kiss, even one hot enough to cause the wet sand around them to steam?

He cupped her face with his hands, running his thumb along her smooth cheekbone. That's when he felt the moisture. Tears. Alarmed, he pulled back. "Isabel, you're crying." He searched her eyes.

"It's because I'm happy," she said with a delicate sniff. But he got the distinct impression that she wasn't happy at all.

* * *

Isabel's family reacted to the news of the impending nuptials with comically predictable enthusiasm. She had been their lost cause, the one they thought would never get married because she was "too damn particular," according to her father. So there was an unmistakable air of relief along with unbridled joviality as the Fourth of July celebration turned into an engagement party.

Craig was convincing as the happy bridegroom, enduring the teasing and the well-meaning back thumps from various DeLeon men with unfailing good humor. No mention was made of the temporary nature of their upcoming marriage, much to Isabel's relief. Her mother might have understood, but no one else.

Isabel, too, kept up a cheerful front as every female in the family jumped into wedding plans with both feet. By the time lunch was ready—a platter piled high with free hot dogs and hamburgers from the concession stand—the plans called for fifteen bridesmaids, including every cousin and several high school friends she hadn't talked to in years. But deep inside, where no one could see, she felt torn in two. It seemed such a travesty of a holy sacrament to be planning a wedding when the divorce was already scheduled.

For the sake of making Sandy her daughter, she would go through with it. And, who could tell? Once Craig had tasted married life and fatherhood, he might come to see that there was nothing for him to fear.

But it wasn't an eventuality she could count on. She couldn't dare hope for too much. Their marriage would be one huge compromise, but at least she would have Sandy. She should be grateful for that, and develop a tough, pragmatic attitude about the rest. Because if she dwelled too much on how good things could be, the eventual breakup would kill something inside her.

The party atmosphere lasted the rest of the day. It was only as night fell and the family settled down to watch fireworks that Isabel had an opportunity to spend more time alone with Craig. Sandy and Corey were asleep on a makeshift pallet under Patsy's watchful eye, so Isabel and Craig laid a blanket on the sand a few yards away from the rest of the family.

"How does early September sound for a wedding?" she asked as the first shimmering ball of pink light exploded in the indigo sky above them.

"Sounds fine. I don't suppose we could elope."

"Only if you want to make enemies for life out of my entire family. Weddings are a big deal. And since I'm the first daughter to get married, it's a really big deal. I'm sorry."

He laid his hand on her bare knee and rubbed it gently. "Don't apologize. I was only teasing. I don't mind a big wedding, although I don't know how you'll put it together in only two months."

"Trust me, it'll get done."

"We can't take a honeymoon, not till Blue Waters is done."

"I understand. Will you . . . I mean, would you mind if we lived in my house? There's lots of room. I spent three years renovating it, and I'd hate to give it up. Although, if you want us to move to Dallas—"

"I would never ask you to leave your beautiful house. And I think I can find enough work down here to keep me busy even after Blue Waters is done."

"Really? What about your company?"

"Sometimes I'll need to be there. In fact, I'll be going up to Dallas for a couple of days next week. But I have a partner who keeps the business running just fine when I'm away. That shouldn't be a problem."

She noticed that Craig didn't mention the possibility of relocating his business in Galveston. But of course, why would he? In less than a year, the adoption would be final, one way or another, and he would be free to return to Dallas on a permanent basis.

"How will your father feel about you getting married?"

Craig's hand on her knee grew suddenly still. "My God, I hadn't even thought about him. Not that it matters to me, but I'm afraid he won't approve. I hope you won't let his attitude bother you, either."

"Why won't he approve?"

"Well, he's very conservative, and he might have a problem with the fact that you're ... that I'm ..."

Understanding dawned. "Oh, he won't like it that I'm not a white-Anglo-Saxon-Protestant."

Craig nodded uneasily.

"He didn't seem to mind doing business with me."

"Oh, that's different. Your bid was the lowest and your designs were the best. Sinclair wouldn't let your cultural background interfere with a sound business decision."

"So I can work for him, but he doesn't want me to marry into the family."

A huge waterfall of white light cascaded overhead, illuminating Craig's face for long enough that Isabel could see the bitterness there. "As far as I'm concerned," he said in a harsh voice, "there is no family. And I don't care what he thinks. You shouldn't care, either."

"Of course I care," she insisted. "He's your father. Did you say you're going to Dallas next week?"

"Yeah..." he answered warily.

"I was planning on going up the week after, for market at the Trade Center, but I could rearrange things a bit and go earlier. Why don't we fly up and meet with your father? We could tell him the news together."

"That's the craziest idea you've ever had."

"Will you do it?"

"Isabel, you are one brave lady." He hesitated, then shrugged. "Sure, why not? I might even enjoy the look on his face. Just promise me that, no matter what he says, you won't let him get to you."

"I'll try and keep things in perspective."

Craig put his arm around her, and she leaned her head on his shoulder to watch the rest of the fireworks. It should have been the most romantic of evenings. They were newly engaged, there was a warm breeze off the ocean, the fireworks blossomed before them in Technicolor glory. Instead, she felt like the unhappiest bride-to-be in the world.

She stared off into the ocean as the incoming tide murmured against the beach. Another flash of bright, white light exploded overhead, and she caught a glimpse of the sand castle she and Craig had built. Waves had washed over it, reducing it to a formless lump of sand. Soon all traces of it would be gone from the beach.

The marriage they were planning would be no more enduring.

# Seven

Tolbert's Chili Parlor, in Dallas's historic west end district, was crowded even at two o'clock in the afternoon. Craig, sitting alone at a booth amongst the clatter and chatter of other diners, checked his watch. Isabel was fifteen minutes late, and he felt uncomfortably anxious about it.

She had insisted on renting her own car when they'd arrived early this morning at Love Field, although he would have preferred to drive her to the Trade Center himself and drop her off before his meeting. He didn't like the idea of her negotiating Dallas's horrendous traffic by herself. After all, this city was a far cry from homey little Galveston. What if Isabel had gotten lost, or she'd had a car accident?

He felt a persistent prickling sensation at the back of his neck, something he hadn't experienced since Tom's death. He knew what that feeling signified, too, and he didn't like it one bit. As Isabel's husband-to-be, he was starting to feel responsible for her.

He knew that was patently ridiculous. Isabel was a thirty-year-old woman who'd been taking care of herself for a long time. But as her husband, he would no doubt be exerting some influence over her life. What if that influence was bad for her?

Maybe he should have insisted he drive her. But he didn't have that right. She wasn't a child. No, she most certainly wasn't a child. She could make her own decisions and deal with the consequences. He couldn't blame himself for what happened to her when she was out of his sight.

But he could worry about her. Husbands were allowed to worry, right?

Why was he worrying about whether he should worry? This would give him an ulcer in no time. He wasn't cut out to be a family man, and he couldn't even explain it to Isabel. If she'd understood, she wouldn't have asked him to...

Yes, she would have. To keep Sandy, she would have married Quasimodo. He hoped the adoption went through quickly. Then they could get a quiet annulment, and she could find a *real* husband, someone who would make a perfect father for Sandy.

The thought was followed by a painful tightening, first in his gut, then his chest. The image of another man assuming that position in Isabel's life made him want to hit something.

How was it possible to want a thing so badly and not want it at the same time? How was it possible for something to bring him so much joy, and at the same time fill him with anxiety and a host of other disturbing emotions?

Craig checked his watch again. Twenty minutes. Isabel must be in some kind of trouble or she would have called and left word that she was running late. He started to slide out of the booth—to go where, he wasn't sure—when he caught sight of her, edging her way through the crowd waiting to be seated. She looked cool as a scoop of sherbet in her pastel, floral linen suit and peach silk blouse. Her hair was twisted into a casual pile of curls that cascaded from the top of her head.

"There you are!" she greeted him as he stood automatically.

"Here *I* am?" he repeated incredulously. "I was starting to get worried about you. You should have called the restaurant if you were running late."

"Craig, I wasn't late. I've been here the whole time, sitting on the other side of the dining room. I thought *you* were late. I don't know how we missed each other."

"Oh." Now he felt downright foolish. "Sorry."

She touched his hand and kissed his cheek, diffusing the illogical anger inside him. "Thanks for worrying. How was your meeting?"

"Went fine," he replied absently as they settled into opposite sides of the booth. "All of the investors are pleased with the sales generated by the Fourth of July party. We're well ahead of schedule with construction, so everything's okay."

A waitress came by and took their drink orders.

"Have you checked on Sandy?" Craig asked, feeling an unwarranted anxiety about the baby, too. This was the first time Isabel had left her overnight.

"Are you kidding? I've called twice already. Both Nanno and Oleta, my housekeeper, are there watching the babies while Angie takes care of the office. It's working out fine."

Craig nodded, forcing himself to relax. "How was market?"

"Great. But first I stopped at the antique mall—you know, that one right across from Love Field?"

He didn't, but he nodded.

"I have this client who's really into Oriental stuff, and I found her these marvelous Foo dogs. And this other booth has these gorgeous vintage linens. I even found some pillowcases for us with a J monogram."

"Are you planning to change your name?" he asked suddenly. The thought had never occurred to him.

"Well, yes, of course. Actually, I was planning to hyphenate. Isabel DeLeon-Jaeger. A little cumbersome, but since my business is DeLeon Interiors, I don't want to drop the DeLeon completely... is something wrong?"

"That seems like a lot of trouble. You'll only have to change it back."

A shadow crossed Isabel's face, as it did any time he made reference to the temporary nature of their pending marriage. But he felt compelled to keep reminding her—or maybe himself—that they had no real future together.

"I still want to carry your name, if you don't mind," she said carefully. "I think husbands and wives should have the same last name. When the time comes, I'll simply change it again." Her voice cracked on the last couple of words. She took a long sip of ice tea.

He nodded, wishing he hadn't said anything. Despite the odd nature of their arrangement, she was obviously enjoying the prospect of getting married. Even if she married again at some point, she probably wouldn't throw another big wedding. He shouldn't spoil it for her.

They talked of inconsequential things as they ate their meal; but the whole time Craig tried to think of something he could do—some small thing—that would bring that happy animation back into Isabel's face. As he pushed the last few bites of his enchilada around on his plate, he thought of something. But first they had to make a trip into the lion's den.

Isabel's eyes were huge as she stared up at the silver-chrome skyscraper that climbed fifty-two stories above downtown Dallas. "This building has your name on it," she said.

"Not my name, my father's."

"I knew he was rich and all, with the jewelry stores and TV stations, but does he own this whole building?"

"Yup. And several others as well."

"I'm impressed."

"Maybe you should marry Sinclair instead of me," he quipped.

Isabel pretended to consider the suggestion. "Hmm, I don't know. How would you feel about me as your stepmother?"

He shook his head. "What I feel for you is definitely not filial." He slipped an arm around her waist and lightly kissed her temple. "Come on, let's go face the old lion."

"Do you really think it'll be that bad?" she asked as they entered the elevator and Craig pushed the button for the top floor. "He won't start throwing furniture or cut you out of his will or anything, will he?"

Craig shrugged, seemingly not very concerned. "With my father, you never know."

Isabel gave a low whistle when they stepped off the elevator into the reception area for Jaeger Enterprises' executive floor. She had worked with some pretty wealthy clients before, but she had never seen any decor quite this pricey. The walls were covered with centuries-old tapestry, and the Chinese bronze statues were museum quality.

The woman behind the intricately carved mahogany reception desk was no less impressive—a pencil-thin blonde who bore a striking resemblance to a pedigreed Pomeranian dog.

"Mr. Jaeger," she drawled in a honey-smooth voice. "How nice to see you again."

"Hello, Buffy. This is my, um, friend, Isabel De-Leon. Sinclair is expecting us."

"But of course. Have a seat, and I'll tell him you're here."

Isabel sank onto one of the plush brocade chairs. She had a hard time understanding how any father and son could be so formal with one another. Craig even called his father "Sinclair" most of the time. He had explained that it would be awkward to refer to him as "Dad" during business meetings and such, and she understood that. But in private?

She wondered what her father would do if she ever called him Hector. And she certainly couldn't imagine her papa making her cool her heels in some reception room. Maybe she was just spoiled, having instant access to him at the diner any time of the day.

"You can go on back," Buffy said after speaking on the phone in hushed tones.

When Craig and Isabel reached Sinclair's outer office, they had to get past yet another secretary, this one older and a bit less decorous than Buffy. She greeted

Craig with enthusiasm, smiled and shook hands with Isabel, then opened the door to the inner sanctum, announced their arrival and ushered them in.

Isabel found Sinclair's private corner office somewhat oppressive, with dark-wood paneling, navy blue carpeting and heavy Spanish-style furnishings, including a rather intimidating suit of armor holding an ax. The man himself was even more imposing here than he'd been in the construction trailer at Blue Waters. Sitting behind a two-ton desk, wearing his somber gray suit and eyeing them both speculatively, he *did* remind her of a lion.

"Pleasure to see you again, Ms. DeLeon," he said politely. Then he turned his attention to Craig. "Well, you've come to see me twice in one day. To what do I owe this honor?"

The tension crackled between father and son. Isabel, a natural-born peacemaker, spoke up. "I was the one who suggested we come to visit, Mr. Jaeger," she said. "We have something to tell you."

"Oh?"

She looked at Craig, feeling suddenly nervous. "You can jump in anytime, you know."

He smiled at her, but when he turned to face Sinclair, his expression was hard. "Isabel and I are getting married. September seventh."

"And we'd be very pleased if you could come," Isabel added, earning a hard look from Craig.

Sinclair said nothing at first. He stared at each of them in turn, as if he couldn't quite make up his mind as to how he felt about the news. Finally he managed something resembling a smile. "Well, I guess congratulations are in order. I'll call for some champagne."

"No, that won't be . . . that is, we really can't stay long."

Sinclair's hand froze over the phone. "I see."

"Mr. Jaeger," Isabel said, "do you want grandchildren?"

Craig's mouth dropped open.

Sinclair cleared his throat. "Well, now, I suppose every man of a certain age thinks about the continuation of his line, that sort of thing. Is there . . . one on the way, perhaps?" While he didn't appear exactly elated over that possibility, he didn't seem particularly displeased, either.

She smiled. "In a manner of speaking. Actually, she's already here, but she's not your granddaughter, yet." Isabel quickly explained how she'd found Sandy on the beach and then applied to adopt the baby. She didn't say that she and Craig were getting married solely to facilitate the adoption; but judging from the shrewd way he looked at both of them, he'd probably figured it out.

"Well, best of luck," Sinclair said. "I hope it all works out. And I'll be looking forward to September seventh." He made this speech in a neutral tone of voice, not smiling, but not frowning, either. Isabel found it difficult to even guess how he felt about all these new developments.

"Ms. DeLeon," he requested, "would you mind if Craig and I had a few moments alone?"

"Yes, she would mind," Craig answered for her. "Anything you have to say, you can say in front of—"

"No, I don't mind," Isabel interrupted. "I'd like to take a closer look at those beautiful tapestries in the reception room. I'll wait out there for you, Craig. It was nice to see you again, Mr. Jaeger. And please, call me

Isabel.'' She shook his hand and then beat a hasty retreat.

*Way to abandon ship, Isabel,* Craig thought as he sank into one of the wing-back chairs opposite his father's desk. At the same time, he couldn't help but admire her spunk. Not many people could face Sinclair Jaeger with such confidence.

"All right, let's have it," Craig said as he stretched his legs in front of him and crossed his ankles, trying to appear nonchalant. "What do you have to say that Isabel can't hear?"

Sinclair made no reply. Instead he rose from his chair and moved to the ornately framed oil painting on the wall behind his desk. With a flick of his wrist the painting swung open to reveal a wall safe. He worked the combination, opened the safe and removed a leather attaché case. This he set on the desk, facing Craig, and opened it.

Craig had seen a fair amount of jewels in his lifetime, but this display nearly made his eyes pop out of his head.

"I just brought these back from Antwerp," Sinclair said. "They're some of the most flawless diamonds I've ever seen. Those clear green stones are emeralds from the Callienda Mine in Colombia. And the light blue ones are Ceylon sapphires. I noticed your intended isn't wearing an engagement ring. I thought you might like to pick out a stone for her, and I'll have one of my designers make a ring for it. It'll be my wedding present to the both of you, how about that?"

"What's the catch?" Craig asked.

"Catch? Dammit, Craig, why does there have to be a catch? Can't I do something nice to welcome Isabel into the family without you being suspicious?"

"Frankly, no. You gave up the right to call us family years ago—when Tom was killed, to be exact. You didn't even come to his funeral."

"I wasn't welcome, that's why I didn't come. I figured I ought to let you mourn your brother in peace. You were more of a father to him than I ever was."

Craig sat up a little straighter. "So, you're finally ready to admit it."

"I've never denied that I was a lousy father. But you were never willing to listen when I tried to explain why."

"I'm listening now."

Sinclair rose from behind the massive desk and came around it to sit in the chair next to Craig's. "It's too late for explanations. We can't change the past. But we can stop repeating our mistakes." He touched the jewelry case. "Take this and have Isabel pick out a stone. Let me do this one thing. And perhaps I can be a better grandfather than I was a father."

Craig laughed without humor. "I don't plan to give you the chance."

Sinclair flinched at the harsh words, and Craig felt a pang of guilt. "Look, Dad, I might as well warn you. Isabel and I won't stay married. I'm only helping her get permanent custody of Sandy. As soon as she does, the marriage is over. So there's no point in getting attached to the idea of being a grandfather, okay?"

Sinclair shook his head sadly. "I guess I don't understand you any better than you understand me." He stood and walked over to the window. Gazing out at the view of the downtown skyline, he kept his back to Craig. Apparently the interview was over.

Craig stood also. He started to leave the jewel case behind, but something made him pick it up. "Thanks for the jewels. I'm sure Isabel will be thrilled," he said grudgingly.

He wasn't sure, but he thought he heard a muffled, "You're welcome, son," as he left the room.

Just as she'd promised, Isabel was studying the tapestries in the reception room. She smiled an uncertain greeting. "Are we ready?"

"Not just yet. Buffy," he said, turning to the receptionist, "is the conference room available?"

She checked a schedule on her desk. "Yes, it is. Just go on in."

"Why do we need the conference room?" Isabel asked.

Craig put his arm around her shoulders and guided her down a long hallway. "You'll see."

The conference room, no less impressive than the rest of the Jaeger Enterprises offices, distracted Isabel long enough that Craig could lay the black leather case on the table and open it. When she turned from studying an original Picasso, she saw the array of eye-popping jewels and her breath escaped her lungs in a loud *whoosh*.

"Where did those come from?" she asked as she leaned over to study the gems at close range.

"My father. He wants you to pick out a stone for your engagement ring."

Isabel looked up, momentarily distracted from the sparkling display. "Is that why he wanted to talk to you alone?"

"That's it."

"And he didn't have any objections to my..."

"Didn't say a word. Funny, I can remember hearing him make all kinds of racist statements when I was a kid. Yet he didn't even seem to notice..."

"Maybe he's changed. Political correctness has swept the country, you know."

"I find it hard to believe he's capable of changing. He's still trying to buy my loyalty." Craig gestured toward the jewel case.

"And maybe that's the only way he knows how to connect," she said in a velvety voice full of emotion. "These are beautiful."

"They are," Craig agreed, softening. Leave it to Isabel to see some sliver of good in Sinclair Jaeger. "Which one do you like best?"

A frown marred her beautiful features. "Craig, I'm not sure I should... I mean, given the temporary nature of our marriage—"

"Your engagement ring will be yours to keep, no matter what happens. And you wouldn't want to hurt your future father-in-law's feelings, would you?"

"Did you tell him the circumstances?" she asked.

"Yes. And he still wants to give you a stone. It means little to him. He has thousands of gems." Even as he said it, Craig knew he wasn't being fair. These particular stones were special to Sinclair. "How about that square emerald?" he asked. "It's almost three carats."

"Mmm, it's lovely," Isabel said, holding the stone up to the light. "But I'm afraid I'm too much of a traditionalist to wear anything but a diamond. How about... this one?"

"You have a good eye." She'd selected not the largest diamond in the case, but certainly the most brilliant. Craig took the stone out of its clear-plastic box, took Isabel's hand in his and laid the diamond on the back of her left ring finger.

"That's quite a sparkler," she said. But her gaze was directed at him, not the jewel.

"It doesn't even begin to outshine you," he said.

"Flatterer." She let the stone slide between her fingers and into his hand. Then she stroked his palm with hers in a circular motion, rolling the diamond between them.

"You want this one, then?"

"Yes." Her gaze settled on his mouth as she moistened her own lips with the tip of her tongue.

Suddenly she was in his arms, kissing him. The diamond clattered onto the tabletop, unheeded, as Craig wrapped his arms around her. He slipped one hand under her lightweight jacket as the other became entangled in her hair, pulling the curls free from their clasp.

Her mouth was soft and pliant beneath his, her tongue teasing and flirting. He slid his hand around to cup one generous breast. He could feel the hard nipple even through layers of fabric, and she made an impatient noise in the back of her throat as he teased the sensitive nub with his thumb.

She broke the kiss, breathing heavily, but she made no attempt to pull away from him. "I want you, Craig. I want to make love."

Her impassioned declaration startled him, so much so that he had no idea what to say. He'd waited a long time to hear her speak those words, and now he wasn't sure how to take them. "If I'd known a diamond would get this result, I'd have given you one long ago," he said, stroking her cheek.

"It's not the diamond."

"I know that." He grew serious. "What is it, then?"

"I guess I was more worried about your father than I let on. I was afraid he would... talk you out of marrying me."

"Isabel. You know me better than that. I gave my word."

"But family is so important, even if you won't admit it. The thought of your father disapproving made me very uncomfortable, and I don't think I could have lived with the fact that your marriage to me had put a permanent wedge between you and Sinclair. If he had reacted badly, I'm afraid *I'm* the one who would have chickened out."

"But he didn't react badly. In fact, he seemed almost pleased—for Sinclair." Craig was still pondering that one.

"And I am very relieved." She pressed the flat of her hand against his chest. She didn't need to voice her desires again. Her brown eyes, dark and soulful, said everything.

Craig placed his hand over hers where it rested on his chest. "Once upon a time, I made some pretty bold statements about making love to you, but that was before I really knew you. I've come to understand that you're a little..."

"Traditional?" she suggested.

"That'll work. And, painful as waiting may be, I'd be willing to wait until we're married."

"Two months," she squeaked. "I may be traditional, but I'm no saint." She slid her hand downward, past his belt, to the front of his trousers. "I don't want to wait, and neither do you."

"Isabel!" He was surprised but not displeased at this more provocative side of his fiancé's personality. "Oh, Isabel." He kissed her again, slowly, pulling her hips flush against his. "Do you have plans for the rest of the afternoon?"

"Well, I *was* going to visit the Designer Showhouse on Swiss Avenue, but I *could* postpone that until tomorrow morning...."

"Then how about a suite at the Crescent Court and a bottle of champagne?"

"Sounds lovely, but who'll share it with me?"

He cupped her bottom. "Certainly not the bellboy." He found the diamond they'd dropped and put it back into its plastic box, then quickly packed up the larger jewelry case. "Let's get out of here, or I might just lay you out on the conference table and have my way with you right here."

He handed both the case and the small box containing the special diamond to Buffy. "Return these to my father, and tell him this is the one we've selected," Craig said, pressing the box into her palm.

Buffy stared after them, openmouthed, as they stepped onto the elevator.

Isabel giggled, and Craig could tell she was nervous, despite her previous show of bravado. Good. She ought to be nervous, given the things he was thinking about at this moment.

Lord, she was something. And he was about to make her his. He should have felt no doubts. After all, he'd been wanting this for months. They were engaged, and Isabel apparently had no qualms about becoming intimate with him.

Why, then, did he suddenly feel like he was about to step into an abyss?

# Eight

It occurred to Isabel, as they checked into the elegant Hotel Crescent Court, that if Craig lived in Dallas, he probably had a house there. She felt silly for not having wondered about it before. "Where do you live?" she asked.

The desk clerk gave them a pointed stare, and she couldn't blame him, seeing as how she and Craig had just checked into the same room.

"I have a little house in Highland Park."

"I didn't think there *were* any 'little' houses in Highland Park."

"Not true. Mine's just a small two-bedroom. You'd like it, I think. It's not as grand as yours, but it's cute."

"Cute?" She couldn't imagine Craig in a "cute" house.

"Well, little, like I said. It needs a decorator's touch. Maybe I'll hire you to fix it up right."

"Mmm," she said noncommittally as the clerk handed Craig a key. Decorate his house, when she knew he would be returning there, alone? Not unless he liked black walls. She would be so depressed, that would be all she could come up with.

"We could have stayed there," he continued, apparently oblivious to her dark thoughts, "but I wasn't in the mood to scrounge around for sheets and towels."

"Not to mention champagne." She pushed her somber mood aside as they made their way to the bank of elevators. She was about to become intimate with her soon-to-be-husband, the most intriguing and exceptional man she'd ever known. She refused to let anything make it less wonderful than she knew it would be.

"The furniture is covered with drapes," he said, "the plants are all dead and the air conditioner is off. By the time we got the place habitable—" he leaned down and whispered the rest "—you might have been out of the mood."

"Craig, a nuclear bomb wouldn't alter my mood." She smiled provocatively at him, her brief sadness pushed to the back of her mind.

Craig groaned and picked up the bags as the elevator doors opened.

A large group of people joined them in the elevator, and Craig and Isabel got edged apart in the crowd. Unable to touch him, she sent him her steamiest look. He shot back a devilish smile, and she could almost hear what he was thinking: You'll pay for this.

Craig had warned her this day would come, and she was glad the waiting was over. How could he have even considered a "marriage on paper?" The sexual tug between them was too strong to withstand a celibate marriage for long. There really was no choice.

And right now, she didn't want one. She'd made enough difficult decisions. Please, just let this one thing happen naturally, she prayed, with no doubts, no second thoughts, and no guilt.

The elevator doors opened onto their floor and they stepped off. With her heart thumping in her ears, she followed Craig to the door and fidgeted while he worked the key into the lock.

The suite was beautiful, done in shades of silver-gray and rose. The curtains were open to reveal bustling McKinney Avenue below, with its trendy shops and restaurants. Fresh flowers and a bowl of fruit adorned a pedestal table. All this Isabel took in quickly, but her gaze locked on the open bedroom door.

Craig set the bags down and came up behind her. He placed his hands on her shoulders and nuzzled her nape. "Should I order champagne?"

"I don't need champagne," she said breathlessly. "It makes me giddy, and I'm giddy enough."

"You can still change your mind." He slid his hands down her upper arms, then down her back to her waist and over her hips.

"You know better." Every nerve ending in her body was screaming for his touch. She wasn't about to change her mind.

"Yeah," he said with maddening confidence. "I guess if I thought you'd change your mind, I wouldn't have asked." He turned her around to face him, his expression more serious than she would have guessed. "Isabel. You have a lovely name. Have I ever told you that?"

"No, I don't think so. Thank you."

He kissed each corner of her mouth, her jaw, her neck. "I don't take this lightly, despite the circumstances..."

"I know."

"I would never do anything to hurt you."

She thought, Yes, you will. You'll leave me, just when I'm coming to love you with my whole heart and soul. "This won't hurt me a bit," she said brazenly as she slipped out of her jacket, then unbuttoned the front of her blouse to reveal a strip of the cream-colored camisole underneath.

Craig's eyes took on the color of a deep ocean as he stared at her. She reached up, undid his tie and pulled it loose from his collar. Still he didn't move.

"Craig?"

He closed his eyes, then opened them again, as if he expected her to vanish. "I'm sorry. I've fantasized about this moment for a long time, and now that it's here, I don't know quite what to do with myself. This just seems too good to be true."

*It is.* But that was the last negative thought she allowed herself. "Why don't you start by...undressing?" She raised one eyebrow and cocked her head to one side.

His response was almost a growl. "I'd rather undress you."

And he did—with agonizing slowness. He finished up the buttons on her blouse, then the ones on the cuffs and slid the silky garment off her shoulders. It floated to the floor in a peachy cloud.

Next he undid the fastening at the back of her skirt, pulling down the zipper at a leisurely pace as he stroked her hips. Wobbling a bit on her high heels, she leaned on his shoulder to step out of the skirt.

He started to pick up her discarded clothes.

"Leave them," she said, walking over to a plush rose-and-silver chair, where she sat down and pulled off her shoes. She unfastened the clip that held what was left of her hairstyle and shook her head, letting the curls fall on her bare shoulders.

She'd never felt so turned on by the way a man looked at her. If Craig could have devoured her with his eyes, he would have. He came to her again, leaned over and ran his hands over the camisole that covered her midriff. The silk felt cool and delicious over her hot skin.

"This is pretty."

"Mmm, thanks. Let's see how it looks crumpled up on the floor."

"Isabel, I never knew you were so naughty." Still, he wasted no time peeling the gossamer silk over her head and dropping it on the carpet. His eyes never left her.

She stood up and wound her arms around his neck. "Finish the job, Craig. You're entirely too slow."

"Maybe you wear entirely too many clothes." He unhooked her bra and freed her breasts. He ran his hands lightly over them as he sucked in a deep breath, then down her ribs and to her hips. With one quick motion, he whisked panties and hose down her legs.

She stepped out of these, also, and kicked them aside. "Now it's my turn."

But undressing Craig turned out to be a difficult exercise, especially when he hindered her progress by exploring her body. She reached for a shirt button and he stroked her breast, all too easily teasing a response from her. It took all of her concentration to perform the simple task of working a button. When she got to his belt buckle, he started tickling her ear with the tip of his tongue.

"This isn't fair," she murmured, even as she savored every sensation.

"And you thought *I* was slow." Before she could think up a smart retort, he swung her up in his arms and carried her to the bedroom. He set her down long enough to pull the covers back, then swung her up again and laid her gently on the pale pink sheet.

He made short work of his own clothes, finishing the job she'd barely begun. Isabel pulled the sheet over herself, more because the room was chilly than out of any sense of modesty, and watched with breathless anticipation as Craig peeled away the civilized layers— shirt, undershirt, trousers—to reveal the dangerous- looking man she'd first glimpsed in the emergency room, when his concern for a helpless infant had brought that fierceness to the forefront.

The teasing banter that had gone on during their mutual seduction stopped abruptly as their eyes met. Craig stood before her, gloriously unclothed. She couldn't name the expression on his face as he came to her. It was slightly predatory, yet not without tender- ness, and it ignited in her a passion so rich, so pro- found, that she felt tears gathering behind her eyes.

He reached for the sheet that covered her, yanked it back and drank in his fill of the sight of her. His gaze wandered from the crown of her head to her toes and back before he finally slid into bed beside her. His body covered hers, chasing away the chill of the room and replacing it with an all-consuming heat.

His kiss was hungry, his tongue a welcome invader in her mouth, his hands roving with shameless bravado over every inch of her. He explored and aroused with clever fingers, and in ways she'd never imagined. They swirled among the dark curls that protected her femininity, teased the crease of her buttocks, danced wantonly on her inner thighs before probing deep inside her.

His touch awoke something that had been sleeping in her depths for a lifetime. She went blissfully insane as he touched all those secret places, physically and emotionally. Trusting him more than she should have, she relinquished all control, allowing him to drive her to a whole new plane of existence. An exquisite pressure built like floodwaters behind a dam that came pouring over the top in a thousand shimmering waves.

When next she became aware of her surroundings, she was clinging to Craig, tears streaming down her cheeks. He held her close and stroked her back, the way someone would calm a frightened wild animal, and her tightly coiled muscles began to relax.

"You shouldn't have let me go alone," she said when she could speak.

"Oh, you weren't alone. I was with you the whole time."

She shook her head. "Not where I went. I was in another dimension."

"Can you show me how to get there?" He leaned over her and made lazy circles around her nipple with his tongue. She moaned, amazed that he could arouse her again so quickly.

Craig would have been content to simply worship Isabel's beautiful body, bringing her to one climax after another. To bring her such pleasure gratified him in ways he couldn't understand. But Isabel, bolder by the minute, wasn't content to simply accept his caresses no matter how much she enjoyed them. She explored his body with more curiosity than expertise, yet her most innocent touch—the feel of her knee against his thigh, the whisper of her breath in his hair—did incredible things to him.

When at last she maneuvered herself beneath him and wrapped her legs around him, wordlessly urging him to enter her, his hunger knew no bounds. He slid inside her silken depths. The feel of her body surrounding him was thrilling, yet as warm and familiar as coming home.

He felt connected to Isabel so completely, in body and mind, that it both excited and frightened him. As he thrust deeply inside her, he felt their souls brush. It *was* like being in another dimension, as Isabel had described it, but this time they were there together.

A disturbing thought flickered through his consciousness, so quickly he couldn't grasp it. And then he thought about nothing. He simply felt, as pleasure welled up inside him to a peak of intensity, cascading over him like molten lava as he poured himself into Isabel. Their cries of pleasure mingled in the heated air around them.

Long minutes later, when Craig felt almost like a human being again instead of something otherworldly, he reached for the bedside phone. Isabel propped her head on her hand and watched curiously.

"Hello, room service? This is room 744. We desperately need a bottle of chilled champagne—the best you have." He paused, listening. "Or maybe the second best. Yes, that's fine." He hung up, then turned to Isabel. "Their best was two-hundred fifty dollars a bottle."

She chuckled. "I see."

"Most people use champagne as a seduction aid. For us, it'll be first aid."

Minutes later, wrapped in the hotel's plush terry-cloth robes, Craig and Isabel sipped cold champagne while draped across each other on the rumpled king-size bed.

"This is true decadence," she said.

"And you seem to have taken to it like you were born with a champagne glass in your hand."

"Mmm, maybe I should have been. If you're not careful, you'll turn me into a lush." She dipped the tip of her finger into the glass, then ran it around the rim, producing a musical note from the crystal. "Craig," she said, a frown line appearing between her brows, "we didn't use any birth control."

*My God, we didn't.* Craig tensed, waiting for the realization to hit him full force. But the only thing to hit him was an odd, totally inappropriate longing to father Isabel's child. What had happened to him? Had sex totally altered his brain chemistry?

But he'd shared more than sex with Isabel. For the first time, he acknowledged what a hell of a time he would have walking away from this marriage. That was the uncomfortable thought that had brushed by him so quickly during the ecstasy.

"We should have been more careful," she said when he made no response. "It would be reckless to conceive a child at this point. Sandy's still so young."

"It would be reckless for me to father a child, period," he said, more out of habit than out of conviction. Isabel stiffened in his arms. He set down his champagne glass and rubbed her shoulders. "Don't pull away from me. This is how it has to be. I don't want to be a father."

"Not even to Sandy?"

"No." He forced himself to say it. "It would be bad for her to become attached to me. I intend to take responsibility for her, but not as her father. As for actually conceiving a child . . ."

"We'll be careful from now on," she said matter-of-factly. "I hear what you're saying. I don't understand it, but I'll live with it. We agreed to certain terms, and I'll abide by them." But there was an underlying pain in her voice that no amount of effort could disguise.

He should tell her about Tom, he realized. Maybe then she would understand why he found it so difficult to accept responsibility for another life. But memories of Tom were depressing, and Craig hesitated to bring up the subject during what should have been a romantic and special evening for himself and Isabel.

*Tomorrow,* he promised himself. Tomorrow would be soon enough to tell Isabel about Tom.

Isabel could hardly believe the past fourteen hours of her life. In one night, she'd learned more about her body than she'd learned during the previous thirty years. She had responded to Craig's touch in ways she'd never even fantasized about.

And he had responded to her. The power they now wielded over each other was awe-inspiring.

Dressed in nothing but her camisole and a lacy pair of panties, she sat across from him, toying with her room-service breakfast and wondered whether they had time to make love one last time and still make their flight back to Galveston.

"You are insatiable," he said, amazed as he spread strawberry jelly onto an English muffin.

"How did you know what I was thinking about? I was actually wondering when I would have time for a manicure."

"You were stripping me with your eyes and you know it." He bit off a piece of the muffin and chewed slowly.

"Stripping you? What's left to take off? I'm going to have to buy you one of these hotel robes, so you can prance around in it half-tied with nothing underneath." She got up and moved around the table, then insinuated herself onto his lap. "Anyway, why would I strip you with my eyes when I can do it with my hands?" She shoved the robe off his shoulder and kissed the sun- bronzed skin she'd bared.

"Whoa, Isabel. The Designer Showhouse, remember?"

She nipped him lightly with her teeth. "I've seen pictures of it. Let's make love."

"We're out of, er, protection."

"Already?"

"I thought three would be enough for one night. I didn't know I was bedding down with an insatiable sex kitten."

She curled up against his chest, disappointed and a little blue that their first romantic interlude was coming to an end.

"Anyway, I want to talk to you about something," he added.

"Oh?"

"It's about my brother, Tom. I told you he died, but now I want you to know the whole story."

Sensing the serious nature of the coming discussion, Isabel wiggled out of Craig's lap and reclaimed her chair, though she pulled it close to his so she could continue to touch him. She laid her hand across his forearm. "I'm listening."

He took a long sip of coffee, and she thought for a moment that he'd changed his mind about confiding in her. Then, abruptly, he began his story. "Tom was born when I was ten. My mother died giving birth to him. Dad was out of town."

"That's a terrible thing for a ten year old to bear alone," Isabel said, feeling for the scared, vulnerable boy he must have been. "Didn't you have anyone to share your grief with?"

"It wasn't so much the grief that was difficult as the burden of responsibility. I was the only person in the whole world that little six-pound baby had. I even named him."

"But didn't your father come back right away?"

"He came back to bury Mom, and then he left again. He wouldn't touch the baby—wouldn't even look at him. I held Tom through the whole funeral."

"Sinclair must have loved your mother very much," Isabel observed.

Craig frowned. "Why do you think that?"

"Well..." She shrugged. "It sounds as if he blamed Tom for taking your mother's life. Why else would he refuse to acknowledge his own son?"

"Because he's a cold-hearted son-of-a-bitch?"

"Was he? Was he that way before your mother died, or did losing her *make* him that way? Grief can be a very destructive emotion."

Craig didn't answer. Had he never before considered the possibility that grief had driven his father? She could see by the way he stared right through her that he was thinking of something far in the past.

"He gave me a pony for my eighth birthday," Craig said. "And he was there. He actually made it to the party. I think he was more excited about that damn horse than I was." He shook his head, as if shaking off the memory. "Never mind. I wanted to tell you about Tom, not my dad."

"What about Tom?" she prompted, giving his arm an encouraging squeeze.

"He grew up without a mother, and he might as well not have had a father. All he had was me. Oh, there were various nannies and housekeepers, but I was the only constant. I bathed him, dressed him and fed him, and later I helped him with homework and fixed his scraped knees."

"So you *were* his father, in a sense."

"I tried to be. But no matter how hard I tried, he didn't accept me in that role. He fought me kicking and screaming at every turn. He got into all kinds of trouble from the time he could crawl. And every stunt he pulled, he was begging for attention from his real father. It didn't matter whether the attention was good or bad—just so Sinclair noticed him.

"Dad spanked him once—I mean, hard, with a belt. Tom went to bed that night smiling. It's the only time I can remember seeing him that happy. But it didn't last."

Isabel knew what was coming. Except for a few minor details, the child Craig was describing sounded just like her brother Patrick. And kids like Patrick and Tom, it seemed, ended up in a bad way.

"Tom was smoking dope when he was thirteen, got kicked out of school for pushing when he was sixteen and he was a coke addict at eighteen. He stole things from the house to support his habit. I got him into rehab three times. Each time he was back on the stuff within a couple of weeks.

"Then he got involved with some two-bit smuggling operation. He was shot at the Mexican border. No one's sure whether it was Federal agents, a rival smuggling group, or his own people that got him.''

"Oh, Craig." He tried to sound unaffected, but she could hear the emotion behind his words. A tear slid down her cheek. She'd had no idea.

He brushed her tear away with his thumb. "I'm not telling you this so you'll feel sorry for me. I just thought it might help you to understand why it's impossible for me to think in terms of fatherhood. I tried it once. I was a miserable failure.''

"You were no more than a child yourself," Isabel objected. "Surely you don't believe you're to blame for the way Tom turned out.''

He shrugged. "Who else? It's hard to blame my father when he was never there, any more than I can blame my mother for dying.''

"Did you ever consider that it might be Mother Nature's fault? Some kids are just born rotten. If you could ever meet my brother Patrick—''

"He wasn't rotten," Craig objected. "He just didn't have the guidance he needed. Anyway, it doesn't matter who's to blame. The point is, I carried the burden of parenthood once, and I didn't like it. I didn't handle it well.''

"Because you weren't ready for it," she stressed.

"I'll never be ready for that kind of pain again. I don't have the right stuff.''

A dozen objections sprang to Isabel's mind, but she held her tongue. Only one person could convince Craig he was ready to be a father, and that was Sandy herself.

"Suck in, Isabel, or I'll never get this zipper up. It's been awhile since you tried this dress on, I take it.''

"Oh, thanks, Angie," Isabel said. They were in her bedroom, getting ready for the wedding rehearsal at St. Rita's Catholic Church. "That's just what I need to hear on the eve of my wedding—that I've gained a couple of pounds."

"I didn't mean that. This is all Sandy's fault. If she hadn't thrown up on your other dress, we wouldn't be in this predicament. Hang on, I've almost got it…there. And why don't you put that baby down before she drools on *this* dress?"

"Because she cries when I put her down."

"She picked a great weekend to start teething. Here, let me take her," Angie said as the doorbell rang. "That's probably Oleta. Thank goodness she was free to baby-sit today. Hurry up, now, or we'll be late to the rehearsal. You've still got to do your hair." She whisked out of the room, baby in tow, leaving Isabel standing forlornly in front of the mirror.

"I thought I'd *done* my hair," she moaned to her image in the glass. So much for her trendy new hairstyle. She went into the bathroom, brushed her hair back and fastened it with a pearl-encrusted clip. Simple but dignified. She wasn't the trendy type, anyway.

The last two months had flown by, and she'd never been happier. Craig, who should have been the most reluctant of bridegrooms, had actually enjoyed getting involved in the wedding preparations. They hadn't experienced any of the prewedding stress most couples went through. It seemed that the more time they spent together, the more they smiled.

Sometimes, in her weaker moments, she could believe that they would stay married. She never pushed Sandy on Craig, but more and more lately he had been picking her up, feeding her, even changing her diaper on one memorable occasion. If Isabel hadn't known his background, she would have sworn that fathering came as naturally to him as breathing.

She heard the phone ring as she dug a pair of white, leather pumps from the back of the closet. What now? When no one answered it, she hobbled to the phone by her bed, one shoe on and one off, and picked it up.

"Isabel, I'm glad I caught you."

"Dr. Keen! Oh, you're going to make it to the wedding, aren't you?"

There was a long silence. "That's not why I'm calling. Isabel, this is the worst possible timing, but I thought you'd want to know as soon as possible."

Isabel's knees turned to rubber and she sank down onto the bed. "Know what?"

"Sandy's mother has been found."

# Nine

Craig hadn't expected to encounter a crowd when he arrived to pick Isabel up for the wedding rehearsal. But Patsy let him in when he rang the bell, and inside he also found Hector, Angie with Corey and Sandy, Nanno and even Oleta—whose position had gradually shifted from Isabel's housekeeper to Sandy's and Corey's nanny. Isabel was the only one not in evidence.

"She's running late," said Angie, automatically thrusting Sandy into Craig's arms—as if a visit with the DeLeons wouldn't be complete without his holding a baby or two. "She had to try on four dresses before she found one that would do, and then Sandy threw up on it." Angie grinned, obviously enjoying her normally sedate older sister's prewedding jitters.

"Here, I'll take Sandy," said Oleta, rescuing Craig from the possibility of a similar disaster to his suit.

"Go up and get her, Craig," Angie said. At her mother's disapproving frown, she added, "It's okay, she's dressed. I think she's talking on the phone."

Craig, feeling unaccountably antsy at Isabel's continued absence, risked his future mother-in-law's wrath and went upstairs after her. He heard her voice before he saw her.

"I won't let that horrible woman within a hundred yards of Sandy!" she was saying into the phone when he entered her bedroom. Her face was drained of all color.

Apprehension twisted painfully inside Craig's chest as Isabel raised her eyes and her gaze caught with his, reminding him of a deer frozen in headlights. She lifted her hand toward him, silently beseeching, and he went to her. Whatever was wrong, he would be there for her.

"All right, I'll listen to her," she said into the phone. "But there's not a chance in hell. Bring her to my house. Let's get this over with." She hung up the phone, then closed her eyes and bit her lip until she drew blood.

"Isabel, for God's sake, what's wrong?"

She took a deep breath before answering. "Sandy's mother has come forward."

"Oh." Craig felt like he'd been kicked in the stomach. "And she wants to take the baby back?"

Isabel nodded miserably. "Oh, Craig, I'm so scared. I've never been this scared in my whole life."

Craig enfolded her in his arms. "Easy, honey. They can't take Sandy from you. This woman, whoever she is, abandoned her baby. She can't just come waltzing in here and expect to claim Sandy after six months."

"Then why does Dr. Keen want me to meet her?"

"I can't imagine."

"Well, he's bringing her over right now." Isabel pulled herself together—dabbing at her tears with a tissue, smoothing her hair and slipping her foot into her other shoe.

"What about the rehearsal?"

"We'll still make it. This woman, whoever she is, won't stay long—I'll make sure of that." Isabel stood, tall and dignified, and marched toward the door. Craig followed, a sense of dread building with every step he took.

"Good glory, what's wrong?" Patsy immediately asked when Isabel and Craig entered the living room, where the others were gathered.

"Something's come up," Isabel said in a carefully neutral voice. "Craig and I have some business to take care of, so we'll be a little late for the rehearsal. But I want everyone else to go on ahead. We'll be there in a bit."

"What do you mean, 'Something's come up'?" Angie objected. "We can't have a rehearsal without the bride and groom."

"Yes, we can," Patsy said, shushing her youngest daughter. There was a knowing look in her eye. Sometimes Craig wondered if Patsy wasn't just a little bit psychic. "If Isabel wants us to go ahead, then we'll go. Come on, everyone."

Isabel threw her a grateful look.

"Do you want me to go, too?" Oleta asked with a worried frown. She'd been planning to stay at the house with both little ones. "I can take the babies with me."

Isabel gave the older woman's shoulders a squeeze. "If you wouldn't mind. But...leave Sandy here. She's ready for her nap, anyway."

Craig was amazed that Isabel didn't send Sandy as far away as possible. "I'll put her down," he offered, taking the drowsy infant from Oleta. He would feel more comfortable with the baby upstairs, quietly out of sight. Isabel kissed her on the top of her head, stroked her cheek, then resolutely turned away.

Sandy didn't even whimper when Craig laid her down in her crib. He stayed with her a few moments, watching her sleep with her thumb stuck in her mouth, wondering how in the world he'd let this baby girl become so important to him. By the time he returned downstairs, Isabel was alone, staring out the bay window to the street. He came up behind her and put his hands on her shoulders. She felt suddenly fragile to him, no more substantial than a dove.

"They won't take her," he said in a low voice. "If there's even a chance, I'll hire the best lawyer in the country."

"Surely it won't come to that," Isabel said in a choked voice. "Maybe all this woman wants is to see the baby. Maybe if I show her Sandy, she'll go away."

Craig didn't believe that for a second. Who could see Sandy and not instantly fall in love with her? *He* certainly had. He could admit that now.

"Here they come," Isabel said as Dr. Keen's Mercedes station wagon pulled into the driveway. "Craig...I'm glad you're here."

He squeezed her shoulders and kissed her cheek. Where else would he be?

They watched, holding a collective breath, as Dr. Keen helped a dark-haired woman from the passenger seat of his car.

"She's so tiny," Isabel observed.

"And young," Craig added. "My God, she's just a teenager." And she was pitiful-looking, dressed in ill-fitting clothes, her hair pulled into a long, scraggly braid thrown over one shoulder. When Isabel opened the front door to admit them, Craig looked into the saddest eyes he'd ever seen.

Dr. Keen made awkward introductions, after which the woman, whose name was Maria, launched into a flood of Spanish that Craig didn't have a prayer of understanding.

"She doesn't speak much English," Dr. Keen said in an aside to Craig. "I had to get the original story through an interpreter."

Isabel obviously had no trouble understanding. She bit her lip and nodded as she listened, and before long tears filled her eyes and she was taking Maria's hands between hers. She said something to the girl in Spanish, then turned to the men and translated. "We're going to sit down in the living room."

Craig could only follow them, shaking his head in dismay. What was going on here? A few minutes ago, Maria had been "that horrible woman." What could she possibly have said that would make Isabel act this way?

They all settled in the living room, the two women on a sofa, the two men in chairs facing them. All the while, the young woman never stopped talking. Whatever her story, it was taking its toll on her. She was nearly hysterical by the time she finished. Isabel put her arm around Maria's shoulders and crooned something in Spanish.

Then she turned to Craig. "Could you get her some hot tea?"

He most definitely did *not* like this turn of events. But he could hardly argue when he wasn't sure just what he was objecting to. So he went to the kitchen.

By the time he returned to the living room with a cup of tea, Maria had calmed somewhat. She took several unsteady gulps of the steaming beverage, which seemed to fortify her. Then she set the cup and saucer on the coffee table.

"Can I see baby?" she asked in English, her hopeful gaze darting between Isabel and Craig. She reminded Craig of a puppy craving a treat but fearing a kick instead.

"Her name's Sandy," he said gruffly.

"Sandy?" The woman perked up. "It is pretty name."

"Isabel, you aren't going to let her see the baby, are you?" Craig asked.

She nodded grimly. "Oh, Craig. You have no idea what she's been through." She turned to Dr. Keen. "Would you take Maria up to see Sandy? You know where the nursery is."

As soon as Maria understood that she was on her way up to see her daughter, she poured out a jumble of "thank-yous" in English and Spanish, then nearly dragged Dr. Keen up the stairs, chattering excitedly.

"Oh, Craig," Isabel said again when they were alone. "Oh, Craig, it's so awful."

"Would you stop saying 'Oh, Craig' and tell me? What did that woman say?"

"She was only sixteen when she got pregnant, and her parents threw her out of the house. She didn't have anywhere to go, so she moved in with her boyfriend, who was a major jerk. He kept trying to force her to have an...an..." Isabel shuddered, unable to even utter the word. "But she didn't, of course. And then, toward the end of her pregnancy, she got real sick, but the jerk wouldn't take her to the hospital. She was delirious with fever, and she gave birth to Sandy at home."

Isabel started crying in earnest as she recounted the tragic story. "Her boyfriend took the baby from her and...and drove hundreds of miles and dumped Sandy so that no one would ever connect her to him and Maria.

"When Maria found out what he'd done, she left. She was sick and had nothing but the clothes on her back, but she left him and lived on the streets. She's been searching for news of her baby ever since. It took her a while because she was afraid she would be put in jail...or worse, that the baby had died. But she finally hooked up with a sympathetic social worker in El Paso who began making inquiries."

Craig felt like a lump of lead had lodged inside his chest. "Is she sure Sandy is the right baby?"

"The dates match up. A blood test will tell for sure, but I already know." Isabel swiped ineffectually at her tears, then looked up at Craig with a watery smile. "Come on, let's go up."

In the nursery, they found Maria sitting in the rocking chair holding Sandy. Isabel just stood and stared for a long time, while Craig watched Isabel.

"They can't take her away from you," he murmured, almost like a prayer.

"They won't have to. I'm going to give her back."

"Isabel, no!"

"Craig, look at them. Really look. Then tell me I should fight to keep that mother and child apart."

He did look. An uncomfortable tightness nagged at the back of his throat. Sandy, who should have been cranky from teething and being awakened in the middle of her nap, was smiling and gurgling. And Maria...her tear-streaked face reflected the serenity of a Madonna.

*"Es muy bonita, si,"* she crooned to the baby.

"How will she take care of Sandy?" Craig asked.

Dr. Keen answered. "She's been living in a women's shelter in Houston, but she has a job and she's getting ready to move into a boarding house. Her social worker says she's doing well."

"But we could give Sandy so much more..." Craig knew, even before the words were out of his mouth, that he was grasping at straws. All the money and privilege in the world didn't amount to a grain of sand when compared to a mother's love. "Damn it, you're right," he muttered, and he left the room.

He didn't go very far. At the stairs he stopped, too weary to continue, and sank down to the top step. Isabel joined him a minute or so later, sitting down next to him.

"It'll be okay," she said in a strained voice, rubbing his shoulder. "Sandy will have love. That's the important thing."

"Yeah." He found it odd that she was the one comforting him, when it should have been the other way around.

"Look at the bright side. You're off the hook."

He turned to stare at her, his desolation giving way to a sharp, painful suspicion. "What do you mean?"

"You don't have to marry me," she explained, her tone falsely glib. "If I'm not going to adopt Sandy, there's no reason . . . right?"

He hadn't thought that far ahead. Again he felt that painful sensation of having the breath kicked out of him. "Well . . ." He hesitated, loathe to agree with her. But what choice did he have? "Since Sandy *was* the main reason we were getting married, I guess . . . we should call off the wedding." He found those the most incredibly difficult words he'd ever said—certainly harder than when he'd proposed. He should have felt instant relief. Instead he was overtaken by a terrible sense of loss.

"I guess so," she said.

"They're waiting for us at the church."

Isabel sniffled and pulled the clip out of her hair, then ran her fingers through the dark brown tresses. "I'm a mess. If you wouldn't mind—"

"I'll go and tell them. I'm sure your family will understand." Right after they tarred-and-feathered him.

Everyone stared at Craig when he entered the church alone.

"Where's Isabel?" Several voices chimed the words simultaneously. Patsy crossed herself and muttered some entreaty to the saints.

Craig took Isabel's parents aside and explained the situation. Hector gritted his teeth and Patsy shed a few tears when they learned that Isabel would be losing Sandy, but they didn't seem surprised to hear that the wedding had been called off. And they didn't direct any anger at Craig, much to his relief.

The brothers, Paulo, David and Alonzo, were a little more vocal in their disappointment, and Angie burst into hysterical tears. The various bridesmaids and groomsmen, most of whom Craig had never met, merely looked bewildered. And the poor priest was beside himself, tripping over his tongue in an effort to soothe his disappointed flock with biblical platitudes.

"Should we go see her?" Patsy asked Craig. "Or would she rather be alone?"

"Go see her, by all means," he said. "She needs her family." More than she needed him, now, he supposed.

He turned and started for the door. Before he reached it, it opened and a stranger stepped inside the church—a short, dumpy young man with long, stringy black hair and a two days' growth of beard. He wore baggy, faded jeans and a yellowed T-shirt with a beer logo. A cigarette dangled from his mouth.

And he reeked of liquor.

Craig started to tell him he'd stumbled into the wrong place when Angie suddenly spoke up.

"Patrick, what are you *doing* here?" she shrieked.

The stranger gave a big smile. "I been paroled, and just in time for my big sister's wedding, ain't that nice? Where is Izzy, anyway?"

Patsy stepped up to him and snatched the cigarette out of his mouth. "You're in a house of God, or have you forgotten what one looks like? And Isabel isn't here. The wedding's off. So just crawl back under whatever rock you came from."

"The wedding's off?" he repeated, gesturing melodramatically. "Oh, this is serious. Maybe I better pay Izzy a visit. She might need comforting."

Those words galvanized Craig into action. He knew better than to wreak violence in a church, but he grabbed Patrick's arm and dragged him outside, then thrust him up against a wall as everyone else followed, tensely silent.

But no one interfered.

"You go near Isabel," Craig said, "and I'll knock your head off. She doesn't need any more grief right now."

"You tellin' me I can't visit my own sister? Who are you, anyway?"

"I'm the ex-groom, and that's exactly what I'm telling you."

"You and who else? Go ahead, hit me. But remember, we got a dozen witnesses and they all have my last name."

"I'd take your side, Craig," Angie called out.

The invitation to rearrange Patrick's face was tempting, but reason prevailed. Craig thought of another tack that might work much better. He loosened his hold on Patrick's arm and leaned against the wall, shielding their conversation from the others. "How much would it take to get you to turn around and leave town?"

Patrick tilted his head to one side, appraising his adversary. "How much you got?"

"I've got the money I was going to use to pay for the rehearsal dinner. Five hundred dollars."

"For five hundred dollars, you'll never know I was here."

Craig pulled the billfold out of his pocket, extracted five hundred-dollar bills and thrust them into Patrick's greedy hand.

"Pleasure doing business with you," Patrick said, tipping an imaginary hat and sauntering off.

Craig turned to face the stares of the entire DeLeon clan. He thought for a minute the tar-and-feathering was back on, until Hector broke into a relieved smile.

"Thank you, son," he said, shaking Craig's hand. In an undertone he added, "How much did it cost?"

"Five hundred," Craig admitted.

"You should have asked me first," Hector said, a trace of bitterness tingeing his voice. "Patrick's disappearing act can be had for two. Can we buy you dinner later on, maybe?"

Craig shook his head. Right now, all he wanted was to be by himself, where he could sort through the day's disturbing events. But he had to clear up at least one troubling matter before he took off. "Patrick is really your son?" he asked the DeLeons.

"We don't like to claim him," Hector said solemnly, "but he's our flesh and blood."

"And you didn't raise him any differently than the rest, right?"

"Patrick came different from the womb," Patsy said, shaking her head sadly. "There was nothing different about his childhood that he didn't bring on himself. Sometimes I still wonder what we could have done differently, but..." She shrugged.

Angie, who had been listening to the conversation, put her arm around her mother's shoulders. "Hey, one rotten apple out of six isn't so bad. The rest of us make up for Patrick, right?"

Patsy issued an unladylike snort.

"Well, most of the time," Angie added.

Patsy gave her youngest daughter a sideways look, then nodded grudgingly. Corey, riding on Angie's hip, reached for his grandmother. Patsy took him into her arms, smiling benevolently. Babies, it seemed, had a way of healing old wounds.

Feeling more awkward by the minute, Craig said hasty goodbyes and headed for his car. He felt very alone as he climbed into the BMW.

Driving slowly back to Blue Waters, he thought about the DeLeons. He'd once envisioned them as the perfect family, but now he understood that they'd weathered storms and had hidden skeletons in the closet, just like everyone else. Angie's unplanned pregnancy had no doubt sent shock waves through the ranks, and God only knew what kind of hell that awful Patrick had put them all through.

Hector and Patsy had lost a child, too. Their first-born, a son, had died as an infant. Isabel had only recently told Craig about it.

Craig pulled his car into the driveway behind his condo, but instead of going inside, he walked down to the beach and stared out at the endless sea. The sun had lowered below the stucco buildings behind him, casting long shadows in the sand.

Isabel had tried to tell him about Patrick, but he hadn't paid attention. Now he wished he had. Maybe he would have understood sooner that some people *were* born rotten. Patrick had grown up in the same warm, nurturing family as the rest of the DeLeons, and look how he'd turned out.

All right, so maybe no one was really to blame for how Tom had ended up, except Tom himself. Maybe even if Sinclair had been a loving, supportive father, it wouldn't have made any difference. And maybe nothing Craig could have done would have saved his brother's life.

Craig *still* didn't want to be a father. Because having children meant taking the risk of losing them. And losing a child—no matter what form that loss took— was too damn painful.

Isabel knocked on Craig's door, ready to give him a piece of her mind the moment he answered. Granted, her emotions were a mess, what with the canceled wedding and dealing with Maria and all, but Craig had *abandoned* her to her well-meaning but smothering family. Just because she and Craig were no longer getting married, it didn't mean they'd stopped caring about each other.

He opened the door after what seemed like a long time, wearing nothing but a pair of jeans. The moment Isabel saw his face her irritation melted. He looked every bit as miserable as she felt, a fact that for some reason reassured her slightly. She wanted to go to him, press herself against him, feel his chest against her cheek and smell the musky fragrance of his skin. But she wasn't sure if she even had that right anymore. Now that they were no longer engaged, the rules had changed.

He mustered a smile for her, causing her heart to ache. "Isabel." He seemed surprised to see her.

"May I come in?" The question came out sounding oddly formal. *This is Craig,* she reminded herself.

"Sure, but there's nowhere to sit down." He opened the door wider. The condo was completely empty, save for a few boxes, a broom and dustpan and an exercise bike. "Since I was moving in with you, I returned the furniture to the rental company. Guess I'll have to call them and tell them to bring it back. They'll think I'm a flake."

His attempt at humor fell flat.

She brushed past him, then turned to face him. "Oh, Craig, I'm so sorry."

"It's not your fault, honey." His arm twitched, like he wanted to touch her, but he held back.

She wished he *would* touch her. She wanted to reach out for him, but she felt awkward about it—more awkward than any other time she'd been with him. They were standing in the middle of an empty living room, just looking at each other.

She turned and walked to the window that faced the ocean, finding it easier to speak when she couldn't see those stormy blue eyes. "Why didn't you come back to the house after you went to the church?"

"I didn't feel it was appropriate to hang around, under the circumstances. Ex-fiancés aren't usually welcome at family gatherings."

"You would have been welcome."

"I needed some time alone."

That, at least, made sense, Isabel thought. "Do you want me to go, then?" she asked, terrified of what he might say.

"No," he answered, almost before she had even finished the question. He came up behind her and wrapped his arms around her, pressing his face against her hair. "I don't know what's left for us, Isabel. We've come a long way, and I can't see going back-ward..."

She knew what he meant. They had already come to think in terms of husband and wife. How could they go back to just dating?

"What are our alternatives?" he persisted. "We've been... we've shared a lot, but I can't see us continuing without benefit of... damn, this is hard."

"Craig, you don't have to explain. I already came to the same conclusion. We've been so . . . so intimate. It would be impossible to go back to hand-holding and good-night kisses, but I just can't see us—me, particularly—carrying on a torrid affair without any commitment between us."

He sighed, and the warmth of his breath tickled her hair. "Exactly."

She swallowed the tightness in her throat and, through the force of sheer willpower, held back tears. She absolutely *wouldn't* cry, not now. "That doesn't leave us with much, except to say good-bye," she said stoically, hoping, praying, that he would contradict her.

But he remained silent. All she could hear was his breathing, deep and rapid.

"Craig." She spun slowly in his arms, so that she was facing him. His eyes were sad, she thought, although maybe that was her own imagination. "Is there any reason we can't say goodbye in our own way?" She placed her hand on his chest and rubbed gentle circles, so that her meaning couldn't be mistaken. She couldn't bear the thought of parting from him forever without loving him one last time.

Craig's eyes darkened with the sudden onslaught of passion, and the air around them grew warmer. "Isabel," he whispered, her name a caress on his lips. He smoothed her hair away from her face, then slowly lowered his mouth to hers.

She'd never felt such emotion in a kiss. Exultation and agony. Pleasure and pain. The musky scent of him, the firm pressure of his hand at the back of her head, the feel of his arousal pressing against her abdomen, all conspired to overwhelm her. She nearly swooned with the power of her own inner fire as it roared to life, threatening to consume them both.

The zipper of the casual sundress she'd thrown on earlier separated effortlessly under Craig's hands. He parted the dress and slid his hands inside, stroking her back, causing her to quiver uncontrollably. Every inch of her skin was sensitive to his touch, sending a confusion of messages to her brain that short-circuited her thinking.

But she didn't need to think. She just needed to let it happen. Craig pulled her dress off her shoulders and down, all the way down, skimming her body with his hands as he laid her bare.

"I don't have a bed," Craig murmured as he kissed a path up her body, across her thighs, her stomach, her breasts.

"Mmm, don't care," she murmured, though words were difficult. Other, more urgent things were occupying all of her brain cells. She unfastened Craig's jeans and worked her hand inside, wanting to feel him, needing the confirmation that he wanted, needed, as badly as she did.

He rewarded her efforts with a tortured groan.

Emboldened, she pulled down his jeans and underwear and did something she'd never done, never felt the urge to do, before: She took him into her mouth, expressing her passion in a totally new way. Running solely on instinct, she sank to her knees and poured herself into the exercise, knowing she was bringing him pleasure, amazed that she could find such enjoyment herself.

"Isabel, oh, Isabel," he muttered. "It's too much." He effectively ended her ministrations when his knees buckled and he sank down to the cream-colored carpet, dragging her down with him. He rolled onto his back and pulled her over him, the hard length of him touching her intimately with only a thin layer of silk between them.

He showed more presence of mind than she did when he reached for his discarded jeans, his wallet and the protection he always kept with him because they never knew when passion and opportunity would come together. But protecting her was the last practical thing they did.

Craig had always been the most gentle of lovers, considerate of her comfort, answering her needs before his own. Tonight was different. Tonight something drove him to the heights of passion, never rough with her, yet fluttering on the very edge of his control.

He held her tightly against him, kissing her with mouth and tongue and teeth as he stroked her thigh and cupped her bottom. Then slowly, he pulled her silky panties down to her knees. Cool air kissed her sudden nakedness.

Her own desires answered his wild calling. She kicked off her panties and straddled him, sheathed him, pulled him deeply inside her...then went for the ride of her life.

She teetered on the edge of ecstasy for what seemed like hours. And then she finally fell, letting wave after wave of pleasure wash over her.

She came back to awareness, sobbing—why, she wasn't sure—and Craig was holding her as gently as he would a bird, stroking her, reassuring her without words.

They lay together for a long time, limbs entwined, silent. Dusk fell, casting the room into semidarkness.

Craig stirred and kissed her tenderly, then made love
to her again—this time with all the sweet caresses and
touching concern she had come to love. It was almost
as if he was apologizing for his earlier, more urgent
lovemaking. As they lay together, joined, rocking
slowly, she smiled, letting him know he had nothing to
be sorry for.

"No regrets, I hope," she said, her voice husky.

He shook his head, staring deeply into her eyes.
"No, nothing."

"You're a rare man, Craig Jaeger. I hope life treats
you well."

"You're an incomparable woman. And I hope you
find the husband and children you want," he said.
Then conversation became impossible as passion rose
again, crested and receded, leaving a warm glow in its
place.

Hours later, Isabel realized she'd fallen asleep. Craig
was curled against her in the chilly room, his head
pillowed against her breasts. He didn't stir when she
moved and sat up. He was sleeping the sleep of a sat-
isfied man.

She wished she could stay till morning. She'd left
Sandy with a dozen or so devoted baby-sitters, all ea-
ger to spend time with the baby before the court gave
her back to Maria, but their patience had its limits.
Isabel had to go home.

She debated about whether to awaken Craig. But
they'd said all there was to say, hadn't they? She pulled
on her clothes and shoes, then hunted around until she
found a blanket. She arranged it lovingly over Craig's
sleeping form. She removed her beautiful engagement ring and pressed it into his palm, curling his fingers around it. Then she kissed his forehead and left.

# Ten

Craig lay on the single bed in the back room of the construction trailer—his old digs—and tried not to look at his watch. But he didn't have to look. It was almost two o'clock, Saturday, September seventh—the hour he and Isabel were to be married.

He'd slept all night on the floor of his condo, slept like a dead man, which was only appropriate. He felt dead inside. When he'd awakened to find himself alone—the only traces of Isabel being the ring clutched in his hand and her lingering scent on his skin—he'd known a desolation so deep he didn't believe anything could ever reach it. A cool rain fell outside, not heavy but steady, mirroring his mood.

Would he ever see Isabel again? His work at Blue Waters would be finished in two months, but he had enough work lined up in Galveston to keep him busy here far into the following year. Galveston was a small island. He was bound to run into her.

Maybe, in time, when the shock of losing Sandy and the canceled wedding had faded, he would seek her out. They could start over. He envisioned the reunion a hundred different ways, his heart beating faster as he fantasized talking with her, touching her, kissing her. And every time, he came to the same conclusion. So long as he was opposed to marriage and children, they had no future together. And even if he were to change his mind... was that possible?

He had to admit, the idea didn't produce the knee-jerk reaction of panic it once had.

But even if he changed his mind, would Isabel have him? The only reason she had wanted to marry him was so she could adopt Sandy, and she hadn't wasted any time breaking the engagement once Maria had shown up. Especially now that Isabel knew just how thoroughly Craig had failed his brother, would she want him fathering her children?

Ah, hell, he'd promised himself he wouldn't think in terms like that anymore. And speculating about Isabel's wishes was futile. She'd ended it. She'd left him, naked and alone.

He rose from the bed, needing activity to cleanse his mind. He briefly considered taking a run on the beach, despite the rain, when a knock sounded on the trailer door.

Hope flared briefly. Who else but Isabel would seek him out at the very hour of their canceled wedding?

But hope quickly turned to disappointment, then just as quickly to surprise, when he opened the door and saw the tall, tuxedoed man standing there, water dripping from his black umbrella.

"Dad? What are you doing here?"

"I thought I was attending my son's wedding. Was there a misprint on the invitation?" Sinclair read from the piece of creamy-white paper in his hand. "September 7, two o'clock, St. Rita's Catholic Church—"

"It's no mistake. The wedding was canceled." He opened the door wider to admit his father into the trailer, although Sinclair was the last person he wanted to deal with right now.

"You might have notified me," Sinclair said as he stepped inside, shaking the water from his umbrella. There should have been censure in his voice, but Craig detected only a note of quizzical amusement.

"I really didn't expect you'd come."

"Well, can't blame you for that. I've missed almost all of your significant occasions—graduations, birthdays. Didn't even make it to the grand opening of Blue Waters, and I was paying for it."

"But you made it to my eighth birthday," Craig said, surprising both of them.

"Ah, yes, the pony." Sinclair shook his head, smiling fondly. "What a hopeless nag that animal was."

"I think it was more of a case of me being a hopeless rider. I was terrified of that horse. I still don't care for horses, if the truth be known. But I wouldn't have let you know that for the world."

"No, you wouldn't have. Tough as an old leather boot, you were. Not like your brother."

The mention of Tom laid a pall over their brief camaraderie.

"You got anything to drink around here?" Sinclair asked gruffly.

"Not any of that twenty-five-year-old Scotch you favor. But there's some beer in the fridge."

"That'll do." Sinclair walked into the cramped kitchenette, pulled out two brown bottles, twisted off the caps, then returned to the living room and handed one of the bottles to Craig. They sat down on opposite ends of the black vinyl couch, and Craig thought what an odd picture they must make—him wearing only a pair of gym shorts, his hair uncombed, beard stubble shadowing his chin. And Sinclair, picture-perfect as always, in a tuxedo.

"So who got cold feet?" Sinclair finally asked.

"That wasn't the case. Sandy's mother was found, so Isabel won't be adopting the baby, after all."

"So she doesn't need a husband, either," Sinclair concluded.

"Oh, she needs a husband. Just not me."

"Why not you?"

Craig laughed without humor. "You need to ask? What kind of a husband and father would I be? Like father, like son, and all that, right?"

Sinclair stared at Craig, his face a mask of incredulity. "You think that because I was a lousy family man, you would be, too?"

"I certainly never had a role model in that category," Craig said quietly. "And I didn't do such a hot job raising Tom."

"Hell, Craig, it wasn't your job to raise Tom. You were his brother, not his father. Anyway, I don't believe anyone or anything could have saved that boy."

Craig nodded reluctantly. Hadn't he recently reached the same conclusion? But it was hard to let go of the guilt.

"As for 'like father, like son,'" Sinclair persisted. "I don't know where you got that idea. Aside from the workaholism we both share, you are *nothing* like your old man. I'm ruthless, stingy and cold and crusty as an old brick. That's why I'm filthy rich. You, on the other hand, are ethical, compassionate, trusting. That's why you'll only be moderately wealthy. Until I die. Then you'll be rich."

"You really believe that?" Craig asked, stunned. He'd seldom heard anything but disapproval from his father. A compliment, even a backhanded one like this, seemed foreign to Sinclair's very nature.

The old lion actually chuckled. "I haven't cut you out of my will—yet," he said, deliberately misinterpreting Craig's question. "Send me on another wild-goose chase to a church in the rain and I might consider it."

"Sorry about that. You want another beer?"

"Sure, why not? What else do a couple of woman-less men have to do on a rainy Saturday afternoon but get drunk?"

And they did.

"That Isabel," Sinclair said as they finished off the second six-pack. "She's one hot tamale."

"I knew I'd get a racist comment out of you sooner or later," Craig replied, his words slurring a bit.

"Oh, hogwash. I don't mean anything disrespectful. I had an affair with a Latin woman once...er, before I met your mother. I've always had a thing for women with dark, exotic looks."

"Then why'd you marry Mom?" Craig asked. His mother had been blond and green-eyed.

"Oh, her. Because I loved her."

Craig didn't know what to say to that. His father had never been one to talk about his feelings, but the beer had apparently loosened his tongue.

"Yeah, your mom hung the moon, as far as I was concerned. When she died, part of me died with her." He flashed a sad, poignant smile. "Tom looked just like her, you know. Same green eyes, same mouth, same hair. More so as he got older."

Had he? Craig didn't remember. But he supposed there was a family resemblance between mother and son.

"I could hardly bear to look at him, it hurt so bad."

Craig saw a pain in his father's eyes that he'd never seen before. And suddenly he understood. Isabel had been right about Sinclair.

Isabel sat at her kitchen table, nursing a cup of coffee and wishing she could just crawl back into bed and stay there. Yesterday afternoon, just two weeks after Maria Fuentas had entered their lives, a court of law had awarded the young woman permanent custody of her daughter. A bailiff had taken Sandy out of Isabel's arms and put her in Maria's—her rightful place.

Somehow, Isabel had managed to say goodbye to her foster daughter. Then she'd come home and quietly fallen apart.

Angie stuck her head out the kitchen door. "Iz? Mrs. Gardner is on line two for you."

"Tell her I'll call her back," Isabel answered dully. She couldn't deal with customers today. She couldn't seem to deal with anything. In the span of two weeks she'd lost both Craig and Sandy. Her arms and legs might have been made of lead, and her heart felt empty and cold.

Moments later, Angie entered the kitchen with Corey riding her hip. She sat down at the kitchen table next to her sister. "Isabel? Are you okay?"

"No. But I will be." Someday.

"You don't look very well. Have you had breakfast?"

Isabel shook her head. She couldn't think about food.

"I asked Oleta to answer the phone. Why don't I fix you something? How about some nice scrambled eggs and toast?"

"All right," Isabel agreed, but only because Angie looked so worried. Her younger sister had changed a lot in the past few months. Once shallow and self-absorbed, she had become a regular little nurturer. At the moment, Isabel was glad. She needed nurturing.

Angie held Corey out to Isabel. "Do you want to hold Corey? You can feed him and change him and rock him as much as you want. I don't mind at all."

Isabel couldn't help but smile, remembering how she had doted on her nephew during that first month, denying Angie the chance to learn how to be a mother. And how Angie, her maternal instincts suddenly roaring to life, had resented her sister's interference. Isabel accepted Corey into her lap, savoring his sweet baby smell.

God, she missed Sandy, and it hadn't even been twenty-four hours. She missed Craig, too, now more than ever. She'd almost called him and asked him to come with her to the courthouse, needing his quiet strength beside her. But he'd already said his goodbyes to Sandy. According to Angie, he'd come over last week, when Isabel wasn't home, and sat in the nursery with the baby for more than an hour.

"What did we do with ourselves," she asked Angie now, "before babies came into our lives?"

Angie, her back to Isabel as she worked at the stove, shrugged. "Wasted a lot of time, I imagine."

"I feel so purposeless. It was amazing I was able to get out of bed and get dressed this morning."

"It'll get better, Iz, I'm sure it will." Angie set the plateful of eggs and toast on the table and took Corey back.

Isabel took one look at the congealed yellow glob in front of her and bile rose in her throat. She jumped from the table and ran to the bathroom. Moments later she lost the little that had been in her stomach.

"Isabel!" Angie exclaimed, standing in the bathroom doorway. "Holy Moses, what's wrong with you?"

"I don't know. Probably just stress. I'm okay." But she didn't feel okay, she thought as she rinsed her mouth in the sink. She was dizzy and nauseated—and pale, she realized when she faced her reflection in the mirror.

Angie gave a little chuckle. "If I didn't know better, I'd think you were preg...nant."

Before she'd even completed the sentence, Isabel's gaze locked in on hers and her hand flew to her mouth.

"You aren't, are you?" Angie demanded. "I mean, knowing you, how careful you are...Iz?"

"No, no, I couldn't be," she said, shaking her head and forcing a laugh. "I mean, we were careful. Except..."

"Except? *Except?*"

"There was just one time, the first time. But surely I couldn't be from that one time." She closed her eyes and mentally counted back the weeks. Ten. Two-and-a-half months. Oh, God.

"Does this conversation sound at all familiar?" Angie asked as she helped Isabel back to the table. She removed the offending eggs from the table, then pulled out a chair for Isabel and one for herself. "Only our positions are reversed. I was the one saying, 'but it was only one time.'"

"And I was the one saying, 'You idiot, how could you be so dumb.'" She shook her head. "It couldn't be," she said again.

"What are you so upset about?" Angie asked. "Another baby! It'd be great, just what you always wanted. I know no one can take Sandy's place, but—"

"Mama would *kill* me."

"She would only kill you if you didn't have a husband. And you'd have one. You know Craig will marry you in a heartbeat if you're pregnant."

Angie was right. He would marry her and stay with her at least long enough to give the baby legitimacy, she thought bitterly. But that wasn't what she wanted. No more temporary marriages. It was all or nothing. Craig would take her and her child for the long haul, or not at all.

She sighed. Craig would insist on marrying her. He would never walk away from the responsibility of a child he had fathered. She didn't really believe he would have walked away from Sandy, either. Or her.

But she didn't want him to marry her because he felt obligated. She wanted him to *want* to stay. She wanted him to love her as desperately as she loved him. She pushed herself back from the table, a plan of action forming in her mind.

"Where are you going?" Angie asked.

"To the drugstore for one of those at-home tests. I have to find out for sure one way or the other." And then she would go see Craig, regardless of the test's outcome.

Isabel stood at the end of a long jetty, staring out at the gray ocean, contemplating its vastness. Actually, she was contemplating what exactly she would say to Craig when she finally got up the nerve to go see him.

*"Hi, I love you, let's get married and, oh, by the way..."*

It was so tempting not to confront him. Then she wouldn't have to deal with his antipathy, or his feigned happiness over the prospect of being a father, or worse, his outright rejection of the whole idea. But she couldn't face having a baby alone. She'd seen what Angie had gone through, what she was still up against. Anyway, Craig had the right to know, the right to decide what role he would play in his son or daughter's life.

But *how* to tell him?

"I have something important to discuss with you," she said, testing the words aloud. "No, no, that's not right," she muttered, then tried again. "There's something we need to talk about."

"Yes, there is."

She whirled around, a startled shriek caught in her throat. Craig was standing right behind her, grinning mischievously. He looked devastatingly handsome in casual, loose-fitting jeans and a shirt woven in muted blues and greens.

"You scared me to death," she said, catching her breath. "What are you doing here?" Especially now, before she was ready? She was in her old sweat suit, her hair pulled back in an untidy ponytail—just like the morning they'd met, the morning they'd saved Sandy's life.

"I stopped at the house," Craig said, "hoping to catch you before you got involved in some work project or another, and Angie told me you'd gone for a walk. Since this is your favorite stretch of beach, I thought I might find you here."

"You came to see me?" she asked, surprised. A sense of elation, probably inappropriate, whirled inside of her. Or maybe that was just the morning sickness.

"Is that okay?"

"It's more than okay. Oh, Craig, I've missed you." She reached for his hand, afraid that he wouldn't meet her halfway. But he did, grasping her fingers in his, squeezing so tight she thought her bones would break. She wouldn't care if they did.

"I've missed you, too," he said quietly. "And Sandy. I've been worried about how you would handle it when you gave her up."

"Not very well," she admitted. "I've been worthless at work. But I'll be okay."

"Maria will let us come visit, won't she?"

*Us?* Was there an "us"? "I'm sure she would if I asked. But, as Angie recently reminded me, I tend to interfere in the mother-child bonding process. I think it might be best if I just leave them to their own devices for a while.''

Craig nodded. "Let's walk," he said. They turned and headed up the jetty, carefully making their way over the huge, uneven granite blocks that led out into the ocean. Isabel slipped once, and Craig caught her, his hand warm and reassuring against her waist.

"I shouldn't have walked out here," she said aloud.

"Why not?"

*Because pregnant women shouldn't take physical risks,* she almost said. Instead, she didn't answer.

"So who was your imaginary friend you were talking to when I sneaked up on you?" he asked when they had regained the even footing of the flat, packed-sand beach.

"A difficult client," she said, grinning, knowing he would see through that ruse. "What did you want to discuss with me?"

"Oh, no, I asked you first."

"But I'm not quite ready," she confessed.

"All right, I'll go first." He stopped and pulled both of her hands into his. "Isabel, why the *hell* did we call off that wedding?"

"I thought it was because we didn't have to get married anymore. I mean, let's face it, I suckered you into marrying me by laying a guilt trip on you. You agreed because you're noble and good."

"You really think I'm noble and good?" he asked, seemingly pleased with the idea.

"You *are,*" she said. "But without Sandy's adoption to think of, I couldn't go through with it."

"Because you didn't want to marry me, or you thought *I* didn't want it?"

She studied him through slitted eyes. "You go first."

"All right." He plunged ahead eagerly, seemingly with no reluctance. "I was disappointed when you told me I was off the hook. No, disappointment doesn't even begin to describe what I've been going through these last couple of weeks. Devastation is more like it. The only reason I agreed to call the wedding off is because I figured you never would have married a man like me if not for Sandy. *I* wanted to go through with it."

Her heart slammed against her ribs, then beat double-time.

"I still want to go through with it," he said softly.

She raised her hand and stroked his cheek, afraid to believe what she'd heard.

"Maybe at first we were engaged because of necessity," he persisted, "but things changed. I started really looking forward to being married to you. And I even started to think of myself in terms of...daddy." By the look on his face, she would have thought he'd just confessed a mortal sin. "Now you."

"Was that a proposal?" she asked warily.

"Damn right it was. Oh, hell, I was supposed to go down on one knee, wasn't I? I can't seem to get that right."

Isabel laughed even as tears welled in her eyes and slipped down her cheeks. She was a heartbeat away from throwing herself into his arms when something made her hesitate.

"Oh, yeah. There was still one little problem.

"Craig, what about children?"

"I want a dozen of them."

"No, really."

"Yes, really. A dozen. Or maybe two."

Oh, Lord, he meant it!

His expression grew serious. "Isabel, I know how important children are to you, and I wouldn't think of asking you to bind yourself to me for life if I wasn't willing to have children." She started to protest, but he held up his hand. "I don't want you to think this is some sort of compromise on my part. I *want* children, no matter how they turn out."

"Mmm, we do have some interesting genes in our respective family trees," she agreed, unconsciously patting her flat stomach. "What if we had one that turned out like Patrick? Or Tom." She tensed, waiting for the pain to show in Craig's eyes, the pain that always came at the mention of his brother.

She saw only a brief flash of sadness.

"Actually, I wouldn't mind a second crack at one like Tom. Maybe...maybe what I went through with my brother was Fate's way of preparing me for something like that. Am I frightening you?"

"Are you frightening yourself?"

He shook his head. "I've thought this through. I want to be a father, and I'll try my best to be a good one. I won't let my work keep me away from home. I'll be there for the kids and for you."

Now he did drop to one knee. "Marry me, Isabel. Have my children. You'll make me the happiest family man in the whole damn world."

Isabel wiped away her tears. "Yes, Craig, I'll marry you." She pulled him to his feet. "But I have to ask you this. Do you believe I love you?"

"Yes."

"Do you believe I want you as my husband, whether or not we have babies?"

He looked deeply into her eyes, and she willed him to see her love shining through. His face, tense with concentration, suddenly relaxed. "Yes," he said, sounding absolutely sure.

"In that case, I have just one more question to ask. Can we get married right away, as in now?"

He appeared delighted by her suggestion. "Any time you name."

"Good. No one bats an eye at a seven-month baby, but if it's born any sooner than that, people might whisper." It wasn't how she'd planned to tell him, but it would have to do.

He stared at her uncomprehendingly for a second or two, and then his face split into a grin. "You're..."

She nodded happily.

"How...when...?"

"The usual way. The Crescent Court, remember?" She tilted her head and lifted one eyebrow.

"Mmm, how could I forget? Oh, Isabel." He took her face between his hands and kissed her soundly. The emotion flowing through that kiss chased away any lingering doubts she might have had about his acceptance of her news. Her body blossomed back to life.

All at once he picked her up and swung her around—gently—in a brief dance of exultation, then set her back on the ground. "Come on, let's get you into a wedding dress and see how many friends and relatives we can round up on a moment's notice."

She took his hand and they headed for the stairs that led from the beach to the street, her heart lighter than it had been for a long time—maybe lighter than it had ever been.

She skidded to a stop when she heard a mewling cry, and a sense of déjà vu overwhelmed her. "Craig," she said, "do you realize this is exactly the spot where I found Sandy?" She looked around frantically, searching for the source of the cry.

And then she saw it. A cat.

"What are you looking for?" Craig asked.

"Nothing. Nothing at all," she replied, resuming their walk. She had everything in the world she could possibly want.

# Epilogue

No holiday passed without the DeLeon clan making a big deal out of it, and Easter was no exception. Everyone had gone to early Mass at St. Rita's. Now the children were tearing all over the big old Victorian house, searching for the hard-boiled eggs Angie had decorated and hidden for them. Patsy and Hector were in the kitchen, preparing baked ham with all the trimmings. A delectable scent wafted through every room.

Isabel lay on the sofa in the living room propped up with pillows, looking pretty snappy for a woman who'd just given birth four days ago, Craig thought. But then, she'd breezed through the whole thing like it was a party.

Craig had been nervous, the memory of his mother's death in childbirth never far from his mind. But nothing had gone wrong. He'd witnessed a new life come into the world, the promise of her future as bright and shiny as a new copper penny. Craig had been the first one after the doctor to hold his daughter.

He'd scarcely held her since, what with all the relatives standing in line, waiting for their turns to spoil the new baby. But he couldn't begrudge little Susannah—named for his mother—all the attention. There were worse things in life than a spoiled daughter.

Surprisingly, the most flagrant spoiler was the baby's Grandpa Sinclair, who'd dropped everything and flown in from Dallas the moment he heard Isabel was in labor and hadn't budged since. He sat now in an antique-oak rocking chair, Susannah in his lap and a contented smile playing about his mouth. He crooned to her in a nonstop monologue, promising her everything from ponies—Craig cringed—to Disneyland.

This was a side of Craig's father that he'd never seen before. But Isabel had been working on him, determined to draw her new father-in-law into her life and open his eyes to the joys of family. Damned if whatever she was doing wasn't working. Or maybe it was just Sinclair's looming retirement and his new status as a grandfather that had transformed him.

Craig sat in a chair next to the sofa, waiting for his turn to hold the baby. In the meantime, he played with a strand of Isabel's hair and every so often caressed her cheek. More than ever, he was coming to realize what a truly magnificent woman he'd married.

An excited shriek from one of the nieces or nephews pierced the calm.

"Looks like someone found another egg," Isabel said, sounding almost as excited as one of the kids.

Moments later, a miniature whirling dervish in blue corduroy overalls galloped into the living room, blond curls bouncing, stuffing a chocolate Easter egg into his mouth. Angie followed hot on his heels, finally catching up with him as he rounded the coffee table. "Come here, you little monster," she admonished fourteen-month-old Corey. "You're going to choke on that thing. Uck, how disgusting." She pulled the half-eaten candy out of Corey's mouth, an action which immediately provoked an outraged squall.

"You've already had two," Angie said as she wiped her son's face and hands with a damp rag. "Look at your cousin Susannah. See what a good baby she is?"

Corey, easily distracted from his temper tantrum, wandered over to stare wide-eyed at the newborn lying placidly in Sinclair's lap. He seemed fascinated by Susannah's tiny hands, at the black fuzz that covered her head.

"Baby," he said almost reverently.

"You were this little once," Sinclair said.

Corey studied the strange old man with the gravelly voice, then abruptly ran off to find some other diversion.

"I swear, that kid never learned to walk," Angie said. "He just went straight from crawling to running. Enjoy the peace and quiet while you can," she added in an aside to Isabel, nodding toward the slumbering Susannah. "At least she's a sound sleeper."

"Yeah, till 2:00 a.m.," Craig said. "Then she's a regular little insomniac." But he wouldn't trade his red-rimmed eyes—badges of courage—for anything on earth.

A noisy squabble broke out in another room. With a resigned shrug, Angie went to find the source of the screaming. Just as she left, the doorbell rang.

"Oh, who could that be?" Isabel asked with a frown. "I thought everyone was here."

"Not quite everyone," Craig said, still wondering if he'd done the right thing by inviting two extra guests. But when the DeLeons and Jaegers had so much love to share—and food—it seemed a shame not to spread it around.

Craig could hardly believe his eyes when he opened the front door. If he had passed the woman and child on the street, he never would have recognized either one of them.

"Come in, come in," he said, opening the door wider. "Happy Easter."

"Happy Easter, too," Maria said with a nod, her stylish tousle of dark brown curls bobbing saucily. She wore a pastel dress that complemented her slenderness, and the subtle cosmetics on her face lent a certain maturity. She was no longer a waif; she was a fashionable young woman.

And Sandy! Dressed in a frilly yellow dress and matching bonnet, she was no longer a baby but a full-blown little girl. Isabel was going to flip...he hoped.

He showed Maria into the living room, his fingers crossed. "Isabel, look who's here."

Isabel stared blankly as Maria set Sandy down. Then her eyes grew large and her hand flew to her mouth. "Sandy!" Laughing and crying at the same time, she held out her arms. "Sandy, come here and let me look at you. Come see your Aunt Izzy."

Sandy clung to her mother's skirt for a few seconds, hesitating, then plunged forward on her stout little legs right into Isabel's hug.

"She's so big!" Isabel exclaimed as she made room on the sofa. "And such a beauty. Oh, Maria, sit down here next to me and tell me how she's been. Is she talking? Does she—" She cut herself off, then switched to Spanish.

"No, no, I must practice English," Maria said. "I'm doing much better, thank you. I have job at a perfume counter in department store. Much more dollars than hamburger restaurant."

"That's wonderful," Isabel said. "You look fantastic."

Maria blushed. "Show me new baby, please," she said, pointing to Susannah still sleeping in Sinclair's lap.

Craig picked up the baby, ignoring Sinclair's token protest, and put her in Maria's arms.

"She is so tiny," Maria said in a tear-choked whisper as she examined fingers and toes, ears, the rosebud mouth. "Was Sandy so small?"

"Almost," Isabel replied. They shared a moment of silent understanding. Then the moment passed, and each woman reclaimed her own child.

Angie came skidding into the room with Corey on her hip, oblivious to the emotional exchange taking place. "Isabel, Mama wants to know where you keep the— Holy Moses, is that Sandy?" she asked, setting Corey on the ground.

Isabel made quick introductions. But there were no introductions necessary between Corey and Sandy. Sandy slid from her mother's lap, and the two toddlers rushed toward each other, meeting in the center of the room, and launched into barrages of baby talk which they apparently understood. They plopped down on the rug together, Corey gently pulling off Sandy's bonnet. Sandy investigating the buttons on Corey's overalls.

"Wow, it's like they remember each other," Angie said. Then she recalled her mission. "Oh, Iz, Mama can't find your eggbeater."

"In the cabinet over the refrigerator," Isabel replied.

"You need help in the kitchen?" Maria asked hopefully.

Angie hesitated, then relaxed and smiled. "Sure, why not? We can compare notes on single motherhood. My Spanish isn't near as good as Isabel's, but we'll manage."

Maria, after being reassured that she could leave Sandy, scurried in the kitchen.

Sinclair rose and stretched. "I think I'll get some fresh air," he said diplomatically, and sauntered out of the room.

Craig sat down next to Isabel and slid his arm around her. It was one of the few times they'd been alone— well, sort of alone, if you didn't count the three kids— since Susannah's birth. Isabel rested her head against his shoulder.

"This is just how I pictured it," she said on a sigh.

"You mean, you, me, the baby?" Craig asked as a warmth expanded in his chest.

"That, too, but I was talking about our house. When I was renovating it, I always envisioned it full of laughing children."

"It's nice, isn't it? Before we know it, this one will be running wild with an Easter basket, screaming loud enough to wake the dead," he said, rubbing Susannah's little foot.

"And all eleven of her brothers and sisters," Isabel added with a mischievous chuckle.

But Craig only smiled contentedly. The thought of a dozen children didn't bother him in the least. The fact that they would be *Isabel's* children, too, made all the difference.

*     *     *     *     *

# Take 4 bestselling love stories FREE

## Plus get a FREE surprise gift!

**Five unforgettable couples say "I Do"... with a little help from their friends**

*Always a Bridesmaid!*

Always a bridesmaid, never a bride...that's me, Katie Jones—a woman with more taffeta bridesmaid dresses than dates! I'm just one of the continuing characters you'll get to know in ALWAYS A BRIDESMAID!—Silhouette's new across-the-lines series about the lives, loves...and weddings—of five couples here in Clover, South Carolina. Share in all our celebrations! (With so many events to attend, I'm sure to get my own groom!)

In June, **Desire** hosts
THE ENGAGEMENT PARTY by Barbara Boswell

In July, **Romance** holds
THE BRIDAL SHOWER by Elizabeth August

In August, **Intimate Moments** gives
THE BACHELOR PARTY by Paula Detmer Riggs

In September, **Shadows** showcases
THE ABANDONED BRIDE by Jane Toombs

In October, **Special Edition** introduces
FINALLY A BRIDE by Sherryl Woods

Don't miss a single one—wherever Silhouette books are sold.

*Because love is a risky business...*

Merline Lovelace's "Code Name: Danger" miniseries gets an explosive start in May 1995 with

## NIGHT OF THE JAGUAR, IM #637

Omega agent Jake MacKenzie had flirted with danger his entire career. But when unbelievably sexy Sarah Chandler became enmeshed in his latest mission, Jake knew that his days of courting trouble had taken a provocative twist....

**Your mission:** To read more about the Omega agency.

**Your next target: THE COWBOY AND THE COSSACK, August 1995**

**Your only choice for nonstop excitement—**

# DREAM WEDDING
## by Pamela Macaluso

Don't miss JUST MARRIED, a fun-filled series by Pamela Macaluso about three men with wealth, power and looks to die for. These bad boys had everything—except the love of a good woman.

### * * *

"What a nerd!" Those taunting words played over and over in Alex Dalton's mind. Now that he was a rich, successful businessman—with looks to boot—he was going to make Genie Hill regret being so cruel to him in high school. All he had to do was seduce her...and then dump her. But could he do it without falling head over heels for her—again?

Find out in DREAM WEDDING, book two of the JUST MARRIED series, coming to you in May...only in